A VERY HERO CHRISTMAS

888-555-HERO #4

SUZAN HARDEN

A VERY HERO CHRISTMAS (888-555-HERO #4)
ISBN-13 - 978-1-938745-68-3
Copyright 2019 by Suzan Harden
All rights reserved

Published by Angry Sheep Publishing
Findlay, Ohio

Interior Design by QA Productions
Cover Design by For the Muse Designs

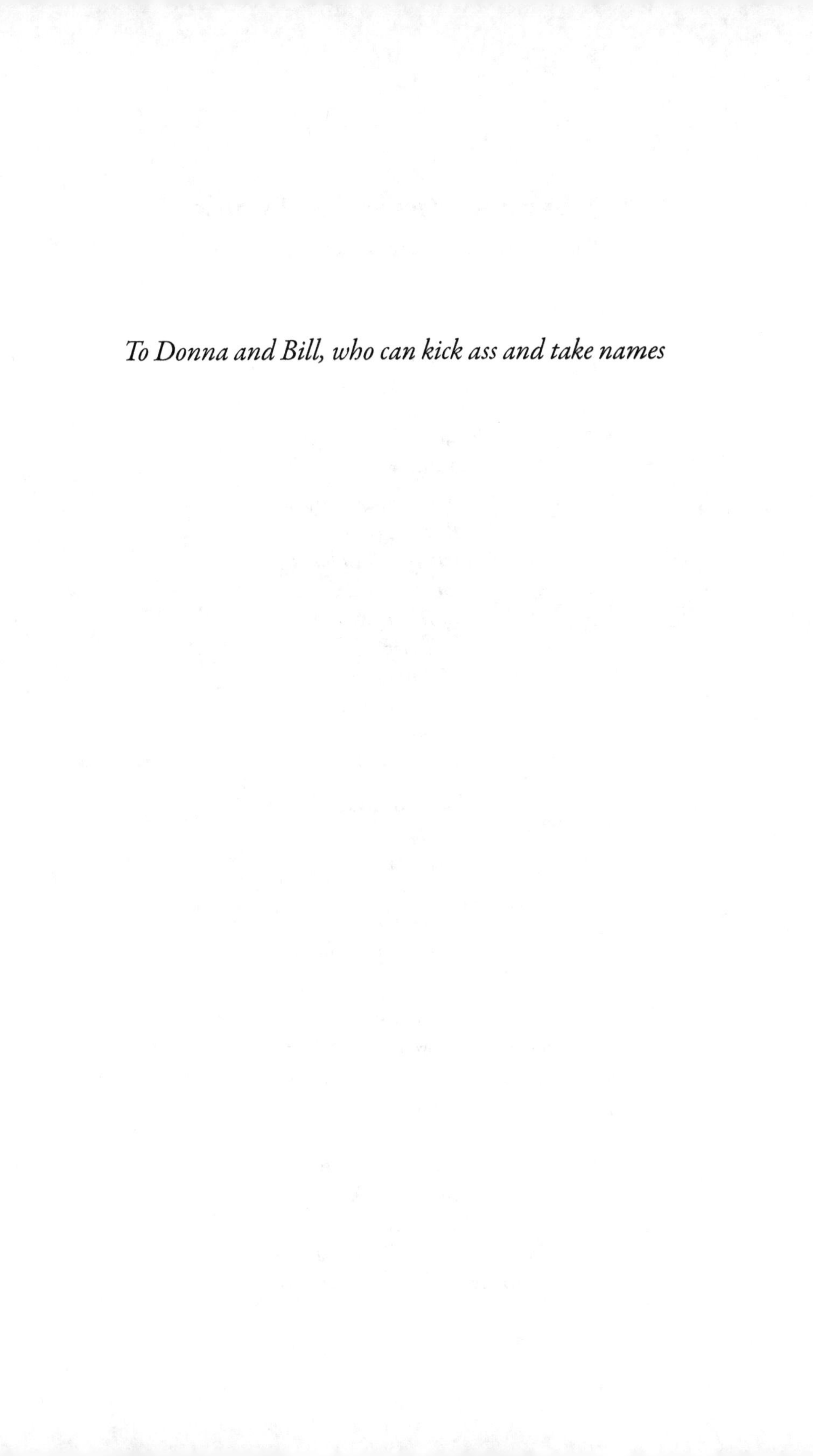

To Donna and Bill, who can kick ass and take names

888-555-HERO
Hero De Facto
Hero Ad Hoc
Hero De Novo
A Very Hero Christmas
Hero De Jure (Coming Soon)
Hero In Camera (Coming Soon)

Millersburg Magick Mysteries
Spells and Sleuths (Coming Soon)
Fae and Felonies (Coming Soon)
Magick and Murders (Coming Soon)

Miscellaneous
Sword and Sorceress 31 ("Pig-Headed")
Sword and Sorceress 32 ("Unexpected")

For more information or to join her mailing list, visit Suzan's website at www.suzanharden.com

Or check her out on Twitter (twitter.com/Suzan_Harden) or Facebook (www.facebook.com/SuzanHardenWriter).

PROLOGUE

Rey Garcia stared at his bride as she lay next to him on the blanket they'd spread on the black sand beach on the island of Kauai. The sun shone against a brilliant blue sky with only the occasional puffy white cloud. Ocean waves lapped softly against the hardened basalt rocks that framed the secluded cove. Aisha looked so damn beautiful and vulnerable at the same time. But she couldn't possibly be serious.

"You can't be the Ghost Owl!" he blurted.

"So, you're saying you want the moniker after all?"

"You're pregnant!" The instant the words left his mouth, he knew he was in deep trouble. And not just from ruining the blissful mood of their honeymoon.

Aisha's dark brown eyes narrowed, and she pushed herself upright. "Excuse me?"

He sat up, too. "I'm sorry. That really came out wrong."

"I seem to recall beating the crap out of both you and Steve when you were under Professor Paranoia's control." Her voice was calm. Too calm. It meant she was on the verge of a serious explosion. Otherwise, she wouldn't have thrown his newly discovered twin brother in his face.

Rey sucked in a deep breath and released it in an attempt to organize his concerns. Aisha would respond better to a logical argument. "I meant we're not sure if you'll keep your powers after the baby's born."

"You were the one with the theory about your mom's kiss protecting me," Aisha pointed out.

"Yes, to protect you *and* the baby, primarily from my uncles." He tried not to think about how Patty's ex Black Death tried to zap Aisha with his powers at their wedding reception. He was pretty sure saving Aisha from little Grace's father was an unintended side effect of Xquic's kiss. "That doesn't mean it'll extend past your delivery. And you had HRSP before you met my biological mother."

The condition known as hormone-related superpowers, or HRSP, often affected women carrying babies with genes related to extraordinary talents. In a large percentage of cases, the condition went away after delivery, but he wondered if his mother had done something else besides protecting Aisha with that kiss. Like making the abilities permanent.

"If I didn't know better, I'd say it was your ego getting in the way," Aisha said. However, the crease between her eyebrows eased.

"If you want to be in the supers business, I'd be the last one to tell you no." He smiled at her. "But I'm not the only one you need to consider in your decision."

Aisha laughed. "Yeah, I've already considered how Harri will react."

"Will you do me one favor before you plan your branding campaign?" Rey took Aisha's hands in his.

"Depends."

"At least ask Tim before you steal his moniker."

She laughed again. "Definitely."

"Are you going to officially register with the NSB?"

Aisha hesitated before she said, "If I keep my powers, then yes. It may be the only way to flush out whoever was feeding Corvus information within the bureau."

Of course. This was more about taking out anyone related to Corvus, especially after Corvus's former leader, Byron S. Trubble, admitted on an FBI wire he wanted Rey and Aisha's son.

Her law partner Harri Winters may have a horrible temper, but it was there and gone in a flash. Aisha had a slower burn, but her grudges lasted a hell of a lot longer. And the fact that Trubble and his people threatened the child Aisha had longed for most of her adult life only made that inner rage burn hotter.

"I'm just worried the NSB will drag you in for questioning about Tim," Rey murmured. He reached up and stroked her cheek.

Aisha leaned her forehead against his and tightened her grip on his hand. "Harri's cover story is holding, and my power set, assuming I keep it, is nothing like the original Ghost Owl's supposed abilities."

She gave Rey a quick peck before she pulled away. "Besides, we need to come up with your new moniker and costume if you want to re-register. But as your attorney, I suggest you forget about everything while you're on your honeymoon. Your new bride is in need of a swim."

Together, they climbed to their feet and raced for the waves lapping the black sand under the hot tropical sun.

CHAPTER 1

Two months later . . .

"The Crimson Commando?" Harri said. She'd lost track of how many suggestions she'd thrown out during this latest brainstorming session. She was also ready to throw a kolache at her law partner when Aisha shook her head.

Again.

And they'd been in their law office conference room for less than ten minutes.

"Too militaristic. Rey wants more of a pacifistic name," Aisha said around a mouthful of breakfast burrito. "Something that won't make the parents afraid. He'd like to do volunteer work like Cobblestone."

"Pacifistic?" Harri threw up her hands. "He's a freakin' demigod!"

"Scream that a little louder the next time," Susan Kennedy said. Their law school classmate, now new associate, deliberately slurped her tea before she added, "Only those with superhearing on this block heard you."

Harri clenched her fists on her lap to keep from pulling out Susan's scarlet ponytail by the roots. Or Aisha's hennaed dreds. "Then why isn't he in here giving us some suggestions?"

Aisha chewed and swallowed her eggs and tortilla. "Who are you really pissed at?"

Harri propped her elbows on the maple veneer conference table. It was bad enough they'd had to go to a used office furniture warehouse. She always thought if she'd opened her own firm, it would be classy. But no, Daddy Dearest managed to blow through the entire Winters fortune.

Or rather snort it.

She took a cleansing breath. The firm couldn't continue riding the fumes of Rey's old licensing deals. "You came up with Captain Justice on the fly after I was arrested earlier this year. Why can't we go back to that if you're going to negate every name I propose?"

"Because you had to bury him along with the original Ghost Owl after the Professor Paranoia fiasco this summer." Susan picked at her banana muffin.

"Not to mention, Jatz'om Kuh was never registered," Aisha muttered.

Harri sat back in her chair. Aisha using the Ghost Owl's Mayan name meant something deeper was going on in her brain. "Is this about Tim? Is he pressuring Rey to take his place? I'll talk with Tim if that's what he's doing."

"No, this isn't about Tim." Aisha laid down her breakfast burrito and shrugged. "Since we learned about Steve, Rey's been . . . adamant about establishing his own identity."

"What do you mean his own identity?" Harri leaned back in her chair and glared at her partner. "Steve doesn't even want to be a superhero."

"Is that the real reason why Rey's been hiding down at Marta's restaurant the last two months?" Susan asked. "He's avoiding Steve?"

"No, Rueben's showing Rey the ropes so he can cover the kitchen while Rueben's in Paris." Aisha took a sip of her pixie barf. Harri didn't understand how anyone could handle that much sugar in their coffee. Even more disgusting, Aisha was currently drinking decaf due to her pregnancy.

"Being a short order cook isn't conducive to being a superhero," Harri blurted. For a split second, it looked like Aisha would throw the rest of her burrito at Harri.

"Rey's sticking with his original plan," Aisha growled. "He's investing in this neighborhood. Getting people working again. Providing them a chance to build real homes for their children rather than squatting in the old Canyon Hotel. That includes sending Reuben to Cordon Bleu for serious training so he can open his own restaurant. I thought you of all people would get behind giving the poor folks a hand-out."

Fury rushed through Harri at the words her father often threw in her grandmother's face. She stood and slammed her palms on the tabletop. "What is that supposed to mean?"

"Okay, ladies." Susan raised her hands. "Let's calm down here. We're all looking out for our client." She eyed Aisha before she turned to Harri. "Right?"

Harri slowly sat down, but she waited for Aisha to make the first move.

Her partner cleared her throat. "Maybe we should table this discussion until Rey, Steve, and I get back from Atlanta."

"After Christmas?" Harri tilted her head. "Why?"

"Because I have a meeting about the new Blue Racer shoe line this afternoon, and I need to get ready for it." Aisha rose and tossed the rest of her breakfast in the trash before she stomped out of the conference room. At least, she'd stopped wearing her damn stilettos now she was in the seventh month of her pregnancy. The office carpet was the smoothest it had ever been.

Susan exhaled gustily. "For being one of the smartest people in our law school class, you can sure be a dumbass at times."

Harri glared at her. "Excuse me?"

"Has it occurred to you the reason Aisha's shooting down every moniker is because she's scared of losing Rey again?" Susan tucked an errant red lock behind her ear.

Harri opened her mouth for a retort, then closed it. She sagged in her chair. "Crap. I hate it when someone else is more right than me."

"She's leaving for her parents' place tomorrow," Susan pointed out. "You and I can work on some names while she's gone. And it'll be a lot harder to shoot down every single one if the client is in here the next time we meet."

"You are truly evil, Susan Kennedy." Harri laughed. "You keep this up, and you may make partner."

Susan pushed to her feet. "How about I survive my first year here before we talk permanent?" She gathered breakfast trash scattered across the conference table and dumped it in the waste receptacle before she turned back to Harri. "One more thing. You and I made the choice not to have kids, but even I can see Aisha's frightened to death something could go wrong with this pregnancy. Especially, since she developed HRSP and is practically invulnerable. Try to take it a little easier on her."

Harri nodded. "I will."

Once Susan left the conference room, Harri stared through the window at the massive gray stone blocks that formed the wall of the building next door to theirs. Aisha wasn't the only one scared something could go wrong with this pregnancy. She sighed. Tim was right. She needed to pull up her big girl panties and quit taking her fear out on everyone else around her.

Maybe it was a good thing she wasn't going down to Atlanta this Christmas. If Aisha was a pain now, she'd be even worse when her relatives fussed over her and the new additions to the family.

Chapter 2

Aisha leaned back in her airplane seat and wiggled her butt in an attempt to get comfortable. Despite all these stupid super powers from the HRSP, she couldn't stop the baby from abusing her internal organs. It didn't help she felt squished in the seat between her husband and her brother-in-law.

"You know, we both offered to get you a seat in first class," Steve murmured.

"How is that going to stop your nephew from practicing his goal kicks on my lungs?"

The plane finally pushed back from the terminal. She glanced to her right. Rey stared out the tiny window. His knuckles glared white against the rest of his tan skin.

She laid her right palm over his left fist. "Breathe, sweetie."

"I can't believe he's afraid of flying," Steve muttered.

"Not all of us grew up with a silver spoon in their mouths," Rey snapped.

"Stop it," Aisha hissed. "Both of you." She glared at Steve. "And it's only when someone else is the pilot."

"I don't need you to defend me," Rey growled.

Before she could call her husband on his crap, Steve said, "You're right, Aisha. I'm sorry."

If her brother-in-law actually meant his apology, she wouldn't have the urge to smack him, too. He was merely trying to show up his twin. Not for the first time, she wished the guys could've worked out their sibling rivalry while they were kids, like normal people.

"I didn't thank you two for coming up to Seattle with me for Thanksgiving," Steve added. "So, thanks for that. I promise to behave myself at your parents' home, Aisha."

Okay, maybe he meant his apology after all.

She eyed Rey.

"I'm sorry for snapping at you, honey." He raised her hand to his lips and kissed the back. "I promise to behave, too."

"Thank you both." After the year they'd all had, a week of rest, good food, and family fun would be a welcome respite from the superhero shenanigans in Canyon Pointe. She didn't realize how much she was looking forward to a real visit with her relatives until now.

Once they were at cruising altitude and the seatbelt sign was turned off, Steve excused himself and headed back toward the restrooms. He pulled out his phone and checked his texts.

Still nothing.

Qiang had a full life long before he met her. Day job, a special needs kid, and elderly parents to care for in addition to her role as a superhero. The reminder to himself didn't check his disappointment though.

He wanted to find something to give to her at New Year's, but nothing he thought of seemed quite right. Rey had known Qiang longer than he had, but the last thing he wanted was to get teased by his twin about his . . .

Steve chewed on the inside of his cheek. His attraction to Qiang seemed far more than a crush or even lust. She was wicked smart, fierce, and a very sweet woman underneath the prickly mental armor she used to keep from getting hurt again.

"Sir, all phones need to be in airplane mode." The flight attendant's smile was polite and firm at the same time.

"Sorry." He turned off the device and shoved it back into his jeans pocket. "It won't happen again."

He turned to go back to his seat when she laid her hand on his arm. "Significant other problems?"

"How did you know?"

"I recognize the expression." A wry smile cross the flight attendant's face.

"More like—" He shook his head at his own idiocy. "Holidays adding insecurity to a very new relationship."

The flight attendant shrugged. "It happens to all of us at this time of year. Give them a chance to answer."

"You're right." He smiled back at her. "She said she still needed to do her gift shopping for her son."

"So she's a parent?" The flight attendant tilted her head. "Then you need to be extra patient. She has a responsibility to him first."

"So everyone keeps telling me."

The flight attendant gave him a rueful smile. "Sorry if I'm dogpiling."

Steve chuckled. "No, you're right. Everyone's right. It's just convincing her that I'm ready to help her with her responsibilities that's the problem."

"No offence, but if she's a single mother, she can handle all the responsibility she already has. She just doesn't need someone promising to be there and not showing up."

"Thank you." Steve smiled. "You've given me some things to think about."

So how exactly did he prove himself to the woman who could do everything?

⁂

The tension eased from Rey's back and neck once they landed in Atlanta. Despite the crushing amount of people in the airport, they found their luggage and their ride in short order.

Rey would have rather sat with Aisha in the rental SUV, but Eric insisted she take the roomier front passenger seat. Not to mention, Aisha's nephew begged to sit next to his hero.

"Have you come up with a new name yet, Uncle Rey?" Even with his seatbelt on and snugly tucked between Rey and Steve in the second row, Devon quivered with excitement.

"Hey, secret identity, dude!" Eric glared at his son in the rearview mirror.

"But we're alone in the car, Dad," Devon protested.

"It's a rental car, and it can be easily bugged," Rey said gently. "The last thing your Aunt Aisha wants would be for you to get hurt because you know my other identity."

"But that's why you waved your phone all over the SUV right?" Devon said. "To make sure it wasn't bugged?"

"Yes, it is," Rey replied. He didn't want to mention he also checked for explosive devices. No sense frightening the boy. "However, we all still need to be careful."

Devon frowned. "But Mom and Dad said the guys who are after yours and Aisha's baby are in jail."

"They are for now." Rey didn't want to get too far into the subject of Corvus either, but neither did he want to lie to the kid. "But bad guys can escape and sometimes, they can even beat the system—"

"You mean, because Cal's an idiot, and he might screw up the prosecution's case," Devon firmly stated.

"Devon!"

What little of Eric's expression Rey could see in the rearview mirror appeared totally appalled at his son's blunt assessment.

In the front passenger seat, Aisha snickered.

"He *is* an idiot, Dad," Devon proclaimed. "He blamed Aisha for not having any babies. And Mom said he was shooting blanks."

Eric groaned. Steve and Aisha laughed out loud.

"Calvin was mean to Aisha after they both promised to love each other forever," Rey said patiently. "That doesn't mean he can't do his job as a lawyer. These same bad guys threatened him and his new family. He understands that no one is safe if the bad guys aren't punished for the things they did wrong."

"You said you'd promise to love Aisha forever, too." The boy peered up at Rey. "Are you going to leave her?"

"No. Absolutely not."

"Have you ever broken a promise?"

"I've only broken my word once—" Rey started.

Devon opened his mouth, but Rey held up his index finger.

"The only reason I broke it is because the monsters who were trying to kill me would have killed all of my friend Takashi's colleagues," he continued. "When to break your word is one of the hard things you have to decide for yourself as an adult. I hope you never find yourself in that position, Devon."

"I hope not, either." The boy nodded solemnly. "Can I ask you another question, Uncle Rey?"

"Sure."

"What does 'shooting blanks' mean?"

CHAPTER 3

In the baking goods aisle of the grocery store, Harri crouched and pulled a five-pound package of flour from the bottom shelf. She straightened and brushed white powder from the paper exterior. "Don't these come in smaller sizes?"

"Actually, you should go back and buy a couple of those delicious-looking premade pies." Jeremy propped his fists on his jeans-clad hips and flipped his longish front shock of blonde hair in the direction of the bakery section of the store.

"No." Harri set the flour in their shopping cart. "This is Grace's first Christmas, and it's going to be perfect."

"Sweetie, Gracikins isn't six-months-old yet." Jeremy shook his head. "She won't remember this. Hell, she can't eat most of what you're making."

Harri ignored him and checked her list. He may be one of her closest friends, but right now, he was being a Negative Nellie, and it was irritating the hell out of her. "I'd better get two bags just in case."

Jeremy slapped his forehead as she crouched and grabbed another package. "Harri, I love you, but you can barely boil water. Put this stuff back, and let's go back to the bakery and deli sections. I know the manager. He'll let us put in a last-minute order."

"No." She crossed flour off her list. "Now, where's the salt?" A sign that said "Seasonings" hovered over some shelves ahead of her cart. Salt was a seasoning, right?

"All of your guests are going to starve." Jeremy threw his hands in the air as Harri pushed the cart down the grocery store aisle. "You may be the best attorney in Canyon Pointe, heck, even the state, but you can't cook, Harriet Matilda Winters!"

He sounded exactly like her ex-husband Eddie. Worse, Jeremy had used the despised full name. She whirled and jammed her index finger into his breast bone.

"I am not going to serve Grace food cooked by maids or caterers like mine and Tim's families did. I am not going to serve anyone warmed up TV dinners like Arthur's parents did. And I'm sure as hell not serving her bread crusts and telling her to be grateful for it like Patty's grandmother did. Grace is getting the real Christmas she deserves!"

"Is there a problem, ma'am?" a voice rumbled behind her.

Harri pivoted and looked up at the huge man, who towered over Jeremy as well as her. His scarlet necktie and white dress shirt matched nicely with his Quinto's Grocery apron. However, his graying beard stood out against his dark skin.

She glanced around and realized she'd attracted a crowd.

"She's just uptight about the holidays, sir," Jeremy said smoothly.

"Is that the case, ma'am?" He didn't have a name tag, but from his stance, the man was probably the store manager. He was also probably worried about violence in his domain. Two idiots had gotten into a gun battle over a fashion doll's dream house at a local chain toy store last weekend at the Southside Mall.

Luckily, Harri's superhero client Cobblestone stopped the mothers before anybody had gotten hurt. Thank goodness, he was still at the store after his annual Christmas gift event for kids in the foster system.

She totally understood why Rey wanted to follow in Cobblestone's footprints, but battling Aisha over a new moniker for Rey was getting on her last nerve. She could literally feel her blood pressure rising, and she shut down that train of thought.

Harri took a calming breath and looked up at the manager. "I'm sorry for my outburst, sir. My brother was merely pointing out I'm being an obsessive butthead over our goddaughter's first Christmas."

"As long as you don't make any more of a ruckus." The manager's salt-and-pepper eyebrow rose, questioning her intentions.

"I won't." She crossed her heart.

"Happy Holidays, then, ma'am. Sir." He nodded to both her and Jeremy before he sauntered back towards the check-out lanes.

With the show over, everyone else resumed their shopping.

"I didn't realize how much the past holidays bothered you," Jeremy said softly as he followed her down the aisle. "Is that why you're trying so hard to be Betty?"

"Betty and Marvin gave us the closest thing we had to a real Christmas," Harri muttered. And Aisha's parents really had been the only ones who gave a shit when Harri and Jeremy had been teenagers. She swiped at her eyes. That damn flour dust was everywhere in here. "Anyway, she sent me a few of her recipes. It doesn't sound that hard."

"Aisha's mom was also up at three a.m. to start Christmas dinner." Jeremy grabbed a canister of salt and set it in the cart.

"That's because she didn't want any interference from Grams and Aunt Queenie." Harri consulted the list again. Cinnamon, nutmeg, and ginger were needed for the pies.

"They only flew into Canyon Pointe our junior year in high school," Jeremy stated.

Harri handed the cinnamon and ginger jars to him. "That's because the Franklin house in this city wasn't big enough with you and I living there. Now, where the hell is the nutmeg?"

"The spices are in alphabetical order, silly." Jeremy pointed at the bottom of the spice rack.

"Gotcha!" Harri tossed him the last jar of nutmeg.

"All right. Fine." He set the glass jar carefully into their cart. "You cook. Leo and I will bring the mulled wine and eggnog."

"It's a deal." She was going to make this the Christmas they all deserved even if it killed her.

CHAPTER 4

When Aisha entered the kitchen of the Franklin family homestead, Aunt Queenie was holding court at the table. No wonder Eric claimed Dad needed help out in the shed, their nickname for the ancient horse barn at the back of the lot, since Rey and Steve could handle all the luggage. From Mom's flustered expression, their elderly relative was driving her up a wall by criticizing everything she did.

"Come here, baby girl. Lemme take a look at you," Aunt Queenie demanded.

"Merry Christmas, Aunt Queenie." Aisha bent to give her a hug and a kiss on the cheek.

Her great-aunt may have been PawPaw's youngest sister, but she ruled the Franklin clan since the day she'd been born. She refused to marry. She claimed she wasn't taking any man's name, but the truth was her fiancé had died on his way home from his service in Korea, though she'd had his baby seven months after he'd shipped out. Neither situation stopped her from breaking a multitude of men's hearts over the decades.

"What's this I hear about you getting pregnant out of wedlock, young lady?" Aunt Queenie peered at Aisha over the rims of her tortoise shell frames. "I thought you were Marvin's smart one."

"I'm married, ma'am." Aisha held up her left hand. Both her engagement ring and her wedding ring sparkled beneath the overhead lamp. "And you keep harping on me, I'll bring up Cousin Eugene."

"Don't you sass me, baby girl." Aunt Queenie shook her index finger. "Stoney and I were married in spirit if not on paper."

She shifted to examine the two men who'd followed Aisha into the kitchen. "And which one of these two is the culprit? Or are you doing both of them?"

"Aunt Queenie!" Mom shrieked over Rey's shoulder.

"The one with the beard hugging Mom is my husband Rey. That's his brother Steve." Aisha pointed in the direction of her brother-in-law.

"Noticed you didn't answer my other question, baby girl." Aunt Queenie's eyes danced behind her glasses.

Aisha crossed her arms and glared at the elderly woman. "That's just wrong, Aunt Queenie."

"Where do you want us to put the bags, Betty?" Rey interrupted.

Thank god.

"You and Aisha are upstairs in the rose room." Mom turned to Steve. "I hope you don't mind bunking in the same room with Devon."

"Not at all." Steve grinned.

"I'll show them, Grandma. Come on, guys!" Devon darted out of the kitchen. Rey shot Aisha a bemused smile before he and Steve followed the kid. Devon acted fairly mild compared to Steve's younger cousins during Thanksgiving.

Aunt Queenie leaned over so far to stare at the guys' butts Aisha feared her great-aunt would fall out of her chair. She straightened and looked up at Aisha. "So, the other one's free, hmmm?"

"You may be a little too much for Steve to handle," Aisha teased.

"Get 'em young and train 'em right. That's my motto." Aunt Queenie grinned.

"We are not having this discussion in my kitchen." Mom glared at them both. "Especially not at Christmas!"

"Calm your feathers, Betty. It's not Christmas yet." Aunt Queenie glared back before she looked up at Aisha. "Grab the bourbon for me and an iced tea for yourself. We'll have a real woman's talk in the family room."

She pried herself up from the chair, seized her cane, and hobbled out of the kitchen.

Mom clutched Aisha's arm and whispered, "Don't let her drink the whole bottle."

"I won't." She retrieved a glass tumbler for Aunt Queenie. A quick look around said they were alone, and she didn't hear anyone outside who would be close enough to see anything. She floated a few feet up to the top cupboard and retrieved the large plastic cup with a lid from a long-ago family trip to Six Flags.

When she touched down on the floor, Mom merely shook her head. "Don't let anyone see you do something like that while you're here."

"I'll be careful." She set the plastic cup next to the tumbler on the counter before she hugged and kissed Mom. "For someone in my condition, flying is safer than grabbing the step ladder."

For the first time since Aisha arrived, Mom relaxed and laughed. "It almost makes me wish I had HRSP when I was pregnant."

For an instant, a flicker of worry ran through Aisha, "What would you think if my powers didn't go away after the baby was born?"

"Baby girl—" Mom reached up and cupped Aisha's cheek. "We'll cross that bridge when we come to it. But no matter what, your father and I love you." She winked at Aisha as she released her. "Just be smart and register if you're going to follow Rey in the supers business. They won't even let family visit vigilantes in the super max prison."

CHAPTER 5

Harri knocked on Arthur's office door and peered around the corner. "Can I borrow your equipment cart for a few minutes? I need to unload my trunk."

Arthur looked up from whatever crap he was doing on his computer and frowned. "Should I ask?"

"Groceries for Christmas dinner."

"Need some help?"

She smiled. "I won't turn it down if you're offering."

Arthur stood and stretched. His lanky form had filled out a bit over the past six months, between eating decent meals and working out with Tim. He pulled a toolbox and coils of wires off the rubber cart and set them on the floor.

Harri led the way back out to her car, Arthur pushing the cart behind her. Jeremy still leaned against the trunk of her ancient white Honda, but he straightened when he saw them.

"Good thing you brought the cavalry," he said as she hit the trunk release on her fob. He pushed the lid up.

Arthur cocked his head and examined the contents. "How many people are coming? I thought it was just those of us in the Lechuza Building who didn't go to Atlanta, Jeremy, and Leo."

"I invited Rue Liberty and her granddaughters, too." Harri unlatched the rear passenger door and pulled a couple of bags from the back seat. "And Miguel invited Marta and her kids."

Arthur blinked. "I understand why we would need extra food." He started placing bags on the lower tray of his cart.

"Speaking of the extra people, would you mind if I used your oven for some of the baking?" Harri set her bags on the top tray. "I can't fit both the turkey and the ham in mine." She grabbed another load from her backseat.

"Not that I mind, but logistically speaking, Aisha's oven would be a better choice."

"I agree." Harri set the second set of bags on the top tray. "However, my super-powered legal partner said if I so much as touched any of her kitchen appliances or her husband's special cookware, she would drop-kick me to the moon."

"Then we won't touch anything in Aisha's kitchen since you cannot survive on the moon without special equipment, and I sincerely doubt Aisha would let you don a spacesuit prior to kicking you." Arthur frowned at the half-unloaded car and then at his fully loaded cart. "We're going to have to make two trips to your loft."

"I told her it was too much food," Jeremy drawled. "But does anyone listen to me?"

"I do," Arthur said.

Harri bit her tongue to keep from laughing. Poor Arthur was so literal.

On the other hand, Jeremy did laugh, but he also patted Arthur's shoulder and said, "That's the reason I like you best, Artie."

Harri expected the former supervillain to correct Jeremy, but instead, Arthur blushed and gave Jeremy one of his rare smiles.

"Is that your superpower?" She grabbed a bag from the trunk and shoved it into Jeremy's hands. "Charming the pants off men no matter their orientation?"

"Why, Harriet, I do believe you're jealous." Jeremy winked at Arthur while he looped the handles of the first bag over his arm. He accepted two more bags from Harri when a familiar motorcycle roared into the garage.

The rider parked next to them, and she pulled off her helmet. It had to be an emergency for Qiang Reilly, AKA the superhero Sparx, to come to the Lechuza Building with Aisha gone. The bitch still held a grudge.

"What's wrong?" Harri asked.

Emotion flickered across the superhero's face, another rarity. "Mom's had another stroke last night. Is Miguel here?"

"I think he's still in his apartment." Harri waved toward the garage entrance into the first floor offices. "We're just on our way up."

Qiang frowned as she peered into the Honda's trunk. "You feeding all the homeless in the Canyon Block?"

"If you're going to stand there and make snotty comments, you can help carry groceries upstairs." Harri thrust a couple of bags at the super. "Miguel and the boys are spending Christmas with us. Is it safe to assume Connor will be joining?"

"If Miguel agrees to let him stay for the next couple of days." Qiang grimaced and followed the guys into the building.

Which was exactly what their maintenance man would do. In a heartbeat. He'd done quite a bit for Rey both before and after the woman Rey had believed was his mother died. But not having her family home for the holidays had to be killing Qiang.

Harri grabbed the last of the bags and slammed the trunk lid shut. Once inside, she set the security system and headed for their antique elevator.

Personally, she thought Qiang was too overprotective of her son. It went way beyond the usual worry over the people in her secret identity's life. Sure, Connor was diagnosed as on the spectrum, but he wasn't stupid, even though he could be as literal as Arthur.

Hell, sometimes she wondered if the real source of the former supervillain's social problems was due to being on the spectrum himself. Arthur's neglectful parents wouldn't have wasted their time getting him the appropriate help. And the more Patty let slip about his childhood, the more pissed Harri became on his behalf.

She entered the elevator and shoved the two gates closed. Arthur pressed the button for the fourth floor. The machine ground to life, and they slowly rose.

Harri turned to Qiang. "How's your dad handling this?"

"Not well." The super shook her head. "He's worried sick. I can't get him to come home and sleep. He's barely eating."

"When Miguel says yes, and we both know he will, why don't you bring your dad over here for Christmas dinner?" Harri shrugged. "Tell him it's just for a little bit for Connor's sake."

Qiang nodded. "That might work. Thanks."

The elevator stopped at the fourth floor. Harri opened the gates. "And if he happens to fall asleep on Tim's recliner, all the better."

"Um, Harri, all of this stuff won't fit in our refrigerator." Arthur gestured at his cart.

"That's because you and Jeremy are taking that up to my loft." Harri grinned. "Qiang and I will drop these bags at your place before we track down Miguel."

"Really?" Jeremy scowled at her. "You're turning us into slave labor?"

"I prefer calling you my beasts of burden." Harri closed the gates. "You're both manly men. I'll be up in a minute."

Jeremy stuck out his tongue at her.

"She won't be up in a minute," she heard Arthur say as the elevator resumed its climb. "She has to fix Qiang's problem first."

"I'm well aware of Harriet Matilda Winters' stunts to get out of real work," Jeremy yelled loud enough for her to hear.

Harri ignored both the despised full name and Qiang's smirk. She charged in the direction of Arthur and Patty's apartment. However, she paused to knock instead of bursting in.

But it was Miguel's youngest Francisco who answered the door. "Hey, Ms. Harri! Ms. Qiang!" The kid brightened considerably when he spotted the super. "Did Connor come with you?"

"Not this time, Cisco." Qiang headed over to the refrigerator with her bags. "Is your dad home?"

"I thought I heard voices." Patty came out from the direction of the bedrooms with Grace on her hip. However, their receptionist's smile turned to a quizzical look. "Why are you two bringing groceries here?"

"Arthur said I could use some space in your fridge," Harri said as she handed butter and cheese to Qiang, who had the appliance's door open.

"Dad's downstairs, working on Mr. Steve's apartment," Francisco volunteered.

"What happened to taking a few days off?" Harri handed the carton of eggs and bottle of cream to Qiang.

"Dad said it was important to get Mr. Steve's apartment done before he gets back because you and Mr. Tim needed some privacy to kiss," Francisco said with solemn surety.

CHAPTER 6

Aisha reached the family room and handed Aunt Queenie her tumbler. Bourbon on the rocks had been the older woman's drink since Aisha could remember. In fact, Aunt Queenie had no problem standing up to the old biddies at church when it came to drinking or dancing. But then, she knew most of the secrets of the rich and powerful in Atlanta, so people didn't mess with her.

Aunt Queenie made a face as she took the glass. "Betty that afraid I'll drink all her bourbon if you bring the bottle in here?"

"You know how Mom gets during the holidays." Aisha settled herself in the cushy chair next to the couch where Aunt Queenie sat. "Everything needs to be perfect."

Aisha glanced out the huge windows framed by dark cherry overlooking the rear of the property and the shed. No sign of Dad, Eric, or LaShun in the back yard. Mom and Aunt Queenie must have really been going at it before everyone from Canyon Pointe arrived.

"Is that why you married the stud muffin? To make your mama happy?" Aunt Queenie peered over the rims of her spectacles.

Aisha chuckled. "No. He planned on asking me from the beginning. Our little surprise just sped things along." She patted her abdomen and would have sworn the baby patted back.

"And how are you handling the HRSP?"

Aisha froze for an instant before she forced a laugh. "What are you talking about?"

"I'm old. I'm not stupid, baby girl." Aunt Queenie glared at her. "Devon already let it slip your man's a super."

Aisha took a sip of her tea. "Devon met a lot of our clients at the wedding. I'm sure he misunderstood."

"Or I did? Is that the story you're going with?" Aunt Queenie made a clucking sound. "Aisha, girl, there isn't any shame in loving who you love, but don't lie to me." She sipped her bourbon. "My Stoney was white back when we weren't allowed to mix. Why do you think my brother and sisters marched?"

"Because it was the right thing to do," Aisha said firmly. She didn't want or need a lecture on family history.

Aunt Queenie held up her right hand. "Fine. But it still isn't proper for you to call your nephew a liar. Especially when I can see with my own two eyes you're having problems keeping both feet on the ground."

Devon raced into the family room. "Who's having trouble staying on the ground?"

"No one," Aisha said. She glared at Aunt Queenie who made a point of staring out the windows overlooking the backyard. "Some people are saying I look like a Macy's parade balloon."

That jerked Aunt Queenie's attention back to her. The older woman scowled. "You are not drawing me in your little fib factory, young lady."

"What fib factory?" Rey stepped into the room. Aisha's heart raced. Three months, and she still had problems believing he was back, much less that they were married.

"Just your wife," Aunt Queenie drawled. "Captain."

"All right. General." Rey flashed her his heart-stopping smile before he turned to Aisha. "Eric and the kids are running to Lenox Square for some last-minute shopping. Steve and I are going with them. Want to come?"

"Are you insane or just from out of town?" Aunt Queenie shook her head. "You can't find parking during normal times at that shopping center, much less two days before Christmas!"

That settled the question. Mom could handle Aunt Queenie on her own. Or she could call in Dad and LaShun for reinforcements.

Aisha pushed to her feet. "I could use some walking after four hours of sitting on that plane."

"Better put a leash on her, Rey, so she doesn't float away." Aunt Queenie snickered in her glass of bourbon.

Rey leaned close to her ear. "You've got it backwards, Aunt Queenie. She's the one who's got the collar on me."

Aunt Queenie slapped her knee and roared with laughter. Somehow, she managed not to spill a drop from her glass.

Devon looked up at Aisha. "Why would you put a collar on Uncle Rey?"

She put her hands on his shoulders and turned Devon toward the door before she gently pushed him toward the exit. "Your uncle has problems with the English language." She glared at Rey over her shoulder.

Damn, if he didn't look delectably wicked with that smile framed by his beard.

Aunt Queenie finally caught her breath. "So, is your brother seeing anyone, Rey?"

"Like me, he's into older ladies, but I think you're more woman than Steve can handle."

His comment sent Aunt Queenie into another round of guffaws that followed them all the way out to Eric and LaShun's rental vehicle.

CHAPTER 7

After putting away the groceries in Arthur and Patty's fridge, Harri stomped down to the stairs to the third floor, Qiang on her heels.

"You know, the offer to start your own accounting firm here is still open," Harri said.

Qiang let out a long, gusty sigh. "I may not have a choice about taking Aisha up on her offer."

"Excuse me?" Harri hit the landing and whirled to glare at the superhero.

Qiang shrugged. "C'mon, Harri. We both know it wasn't your idea. You're still pissed Seismic Shift extorted me into trying to kill you last spring."

"And we both know you're holding a grudge because a mere mortal got the better of you in that fight." Harri smiled sweetly.

"You're right." Qiang's tone was deceptively mild. "I hesitated because I never killed anyone before."

"So, you're trying to cover by saying you took it easy on me?" Harri looked askance at the super.

"All I'm saying is I won't hesitate the next time."

"The next time?"

Qiang merely smiled and pulled open the stairwell door to the third-floor. Banging, rasping, and music filled the hallway.

From the noise level, it wasn't hard to find which section Miguel worked on. Harri poked her head past the drop cloth covering the doorway. The sharp odor of powdered gypsum tinged the air. Miguel's third son Javier and a girl roughly the same age, who Harri recognized as one of the squatters in the condemned Canyon Hotel, sanded the spackle already on the drywall. Both kids wore eye protection and masks to keep the dust at bay.

Javier spotted Harri and lowered the hand sander. "Hey, Ms. Harri." His voice was muffled by the mask, but with the amount of dust in the air, she didn't blame the thirteen-year-old for not removing it.

"Can you grab your dad for a second, please? Qiang needs to speak with him."

The boy's dark eyes turned serious. "Is everything okay with Connor?"

Harri had been a little surprised how quickly Javier had taken Qiang's son under his wing. She remembered from her own childhood how cruel kids could be when someone was different from everyone else.

"Connor's fine." Qiang grinned. "And no one's in trouble."

"*Uno momento*." He set down his sander and ran into the next room.

As promised, Miguel stepped into the room a moment later. Like Javier and the girl, Miguel wore eye protection and a mask to keep out the dust, but his cap and clothing were dotted with fresh spackle as well.

"*Que pasa*, Harri?"

She inclined her head to the hallway, and he followed her.

"Hey, Miguel." Qiang's cheeks flushed, but she kept her composure. "I hate asking for a favor this close to the holidays—"

"Connor is more than welcome to stay with me." Miguel pulled down his mask and pushed up his goggles. "Your mother again?"

The tough superhero's eyes watered, and she nodded.

"Where is he now?" Miguel asked.

"Oliver came over last night, but they're all heading up to Larry's parents tonight for the holidays. I can't ask him to stay in Canyon Pointe. I know he won't see his grandparents that much with his scholarship at UNC next fall."

Oliver, the Northside High School senior who lived next door to Qiang, had been a blessing to her. He understood and bonded with Connor. Harri didn't have a clue of what the super would do when Oliver headed off to college next year. No wonder she seemed so overwhelmed.

Miguel pursed his mouth for a moment. "Let me get cleaned up, and I'll meet you over at your place."

"Thank you, Miguel." Qiang bobbed her head. "I'll have him packed and ready."

"Why don't I stop by your place later tonight?" Harri said. "I can pick up his presents from you so they're here when he wakes up Christmas morning."

Qiang sagged. "I haven't had a chance to finish shopping for him yet."

"Then give me the list," Harri said. "Besides, Tim's been obsessively wrapping for everyone." She rolled her eyes.

"It's the first holiday with his new family." Miguel grinned. "He has a lot of holiday spirit he's buried for the last twenty years."

"Speaking of holiday spirit, what the hell are you telling Francisco about Tim and me?" Harri propped her fists on her hips.

"I beg your pardon?" Miguel pulled off his goggles and baseball cap and scratched the back of his head. Dust flew in all directions.

"Something about you're trying to finish Steve's apartment so Tim and I can kiss?"

Miguel chuckled. "All I said was you need some privacy."

Harri snorted. "No, Steve's going to need the privacy when he starts law school in two weeks." Not that she minded Rey's twin using her guest bedroom. She was getting a free legal intern out of the deal. But it would be nice to have some intimate time with her boyfriend without someone with superhearing in the next bedroom.

"Will you have his apartment done before classes start?" Qiang asked. Her cheeks flushed any time Steve was mentioned. Everyone noticed the two of them were spending time together whenever Qiang could. Which hadn't been much lately with everything going on in her life.

And both Rey and Aisha had promised to leave Harri dangling from the Action 12! transmission tower if she said one word about Steve and Qiang's nascent relationship. When Harri asked Tim why he didn't defend her, he said, "You're lucky I don't have superpowers, or I'd do the same thing."

Miguel nodded at Qiang's original question. The thoughtful expression on his face meant he calculated labor estimates in his head. "We'll be cutting it close, but with Rey and Steve doing the heavy lifting for the cabinets and appliances when they get back from Atlanta, we should make it."

Harri glanced around the hallway. "The next project may be offices for Qiang."

"I didn't say yes," the superhero snapped.

"If we have them ready, and you don't leave your firm, we can always rent them out to someone else." Harri shrugged.

"What about another apartment on this floor?" Miguel asked.

"I'm not joining your little commune," Qiang bit out.

"It's not a commune," Harri protested.

"And it's definitely not little." Miguel grinned. "Think about it, *mi amiga*. When Oliver leaves next fall, being here would be convenient for both your parents and Connor. You have some help here."

Qiang shook her head. "You're worse than Harri." But from the contemplative gleam in her dark eyes, she was thinking about the future.

Harri clapped her hands once. "All right. For now, we plan on the Reilly clan for Christmas dinner, and we leave everything else until after the holidays. Give your people a break, Miguel, so they can get their own Christmas prep done."

Because dammit, she was going to make this the best Christmas for her new-found family. Even if it killed her.

Which at this rate, it probably would.

CHAPTER 8

Aisha sighed with relief as she slid out of the backseat of Eric's rental SUV. Her brother-in-law had circled the mall three times, looking for a parking spot until Rey insisted on paying for the valet service. If it wouldn't cause twenty million other problems, she would have simply flown here.

"You okay?" Rey whispered, taking her hand.

"Just a sore backside." She chuckled.

On the other side of the vehicle, Eric vowed to make the poor valet driver pay in blood if he put so much as a thumbprint on the SUV.

"Dad gets weird about rentals," Jada whispered. "Mom says he needs to just buy the insurance."

"And that's just another way companies rip you off, young lady," Eric said as he joined them.

Jada rolled her eyes, a gesture that reminded Aisha too much of LaShun at the same age.

"What's the game plan?" Steve asked as they entered the mall.

"I need to pick up an order," Eric said. His cagey manner meant the package was for his wife.

"Uncle Rey, can you go with me to get Mister Spectacular's autograph?" Devon looked up with huge, pleading eyes. "He only does signings for charity here at Christmas."

"Devon!" Jada glared at her brother. "What about our present for the baby?"

"We'll get that, too," Devon soothed.

"I am not giving a picture with a superhero," Jada hissed. Her words registered a split second later, and she nervously looked at Rey. "I'm sorry. I didn't mean—"

Aisha placed her hand on the girl's shoulder. "It's okay, sweetie. Let's head down to the signing with Rey and Devon. Then we'll go with you to get the baby's present."

"But I wanted it to be a surprise." Jada crossed her arms and pouted.

If Aisha didn't love her niece to bits, she would have yelled at her for acting like LaShun.

"Was it supposed to be a surprise to me?" Eric gave the girl a look that meant she was on the edge of being in big trouble. The last thing Aisha wanted was a family battle in public, but then, Eric had handled LaShun for the last fifteen years.

Jada opened her mouth, then closed it and nodded.

"Young lady, what have I said about you two running off by yourselves?"

Jada stared at the floor and kicked the tile. "That no one cares about black kids disappearing, and that we need to be smart."

"So, what makes you think I would have let you take off through the mall without an adult?" Eric crossed his arms, but he sounded more tired than angry.

"We were just going to the North Pole," Jada murmured. "It's down the hall from Tiffany's, so I figured we could get our pictures with Santa and be back before you were done there."

"A picture of you two with Santa?" Aisha said. "That's what you're getting the baby?"

Jada nodded, though she still stared at the floor. "I wanted him to know what Devon and I look like." She sniffed and swiped her nose with her sweatshirt sleeve. "We only get to see you a couple of times a year."

"Oh, sweetie." Aisha hugged her niece tight against her side. "I appreciate the thought, and Rey and I really want our baby to get to know his cousins. But your dad's right. No present is worth yours and Devon's safety. Okay?"

"You promise to come visit us once he's born?" Jada shyly looked up at her.

"As soon as our doctor says it's okay." Aisha gently squeezed her niece's shoulder.

"Besides," Devon added. "They've got a whole building now, and we can stay at Canyon Pointe more often!"

Eric groaned. "Before you two plan out the next couple of years, can we get through this Christmas first?"

Steve clapped him on the shoulder. "I'll go with you, and Aisha and Rey can herd the munchkins."

"Behave." Eric waggled a finger at the kids. "If you don't—"

"We'll get coal in our stockings." Devon sagged and swung his arms. "We know the drill, Dad."

Eric shook his head before he and Steve joined the foot traffic heading in the opposite direction.

Rey frowned as he watched the two men. "What's that all about?"

Aisha chuckled while they started following the signs regarding Mister Spectacular's appearance. "I'd say Qiang might be getting something very nice in her stocking this year."

"He's not getting her a ring, is he?" Rey said under his breath. "That's awfully fast."

Aisha looked up at him. "Pot needs to keep his damn mouth shut about speedy relationships."

"That's not what I—" Rey grimaced, and his nostrils flared. "I don't want him to hurt her. I like Qiang."

"Would you prefer he dated Aunt Queenie?" She grinned up at him.

"Very funny. He should be focusing on school—" A scared expression flashed across Rey's face. "Oh, my god. I'm turning into Harri."

"Don't worry." Aisha twined her fingers in his and squeezed. "Jeremy and I will keep you in line."

Rey groaned. "Then I'm doomed."

CHAPTER 9

After letting Qiang out of the building and resetting the alarm, Harri jogged up to the top floor. A pleased feeling spread through her. She wasn't huffing and puffing nearly as bad at the five-story climb as she had when she and Aisha first looked at the Lechuza Building back in May. Maybe those morning workouts with Tim were worth the lack of sleep after all.

Harri's phone rang as she entered her loft, and she pulled the device from the front pocket of her jeans. A frown tugged her mouth at the sight of their associate's cell number on her caller ID.

"Susan? What's up?"

"Harri? I need a big favor." Susan sounded on the verge of tears. "First, please tell me Aisha and the twins are still in Atlanta."

"They are. What's wrong?"

Jeremy leaned on the counter while Arthur folded the last of Harri's reusable bags. Both men paid close attention to her side of the conversation.

"I think someone broke into Mom and Dad's cabin."

A chill stole through Harri. "Someone? As in those pesky birds we've been having problems with?"

With the FBI raids in September, nearly everyone associated with the black ops agency known as Corvus were in holding cells awaiting trial while different federal organizations battled over who was to blame for them going amuck. But knowing Corvus's leader, retired General Byron S. Trubble, he probably had agents and backup contingencies no one knew about. And he made no secret that he blamed the staff and clients of Winters & Franklin for Corvus's downfall.

Especially Harri.

"Maybe." Susan's gulp was audible through their connection. "Or it could be local kids making mischief. The place is torn up, and whoever did this turned the heat off and opened all the windows and doors. Plus, they stopped up the drains and left the water running." Her voice lowered. "Mom's not handling this well."

Crap, that explained why Susan was asking about extra space. Mrs. Kennedy's doctors suspected she was in the beginning stages of dementia. The physicians stressed the importance of familiarity, but Susan was obviously worried. If Corvus was behind the mess at the Kennedy family mountain cabin, they could have laid traps at the homes of Susan's parents and sister.

"Don't worry about it," Harri said. "Deal with the sheriff and insurance today. Find a motel—"

"No." There was some rustling at the other end before Susan spoke again in a lower voice. "My brother-in-law and I agreed. We're heading back to Canyon Pointe tonight while we can. Neither of us want to take a chance we're hit at a place we're unfamiliar with."

Which meant Susan had been straight with her sister and brother-in-law about the Corvus situation, even if she hadn't told the truth to her parents.

Harri's brain was already going through scenarios, and which of their clients she could call despite the holidays. "Driving through the mountains at night isn't exactly a good idea either. Do I need to send you an escort?"

"No. I'm not ruining anyone else's holiday." Susan was silent for a few seconds before she said, "Have you heard from Aisha?"

Susan's words turned the chill in Harri's spine into a frozen rod. "Just a couple of texts to say they landed safely and they made it to the Franklins' house okay. I'll double-check to make sure."

"We'll be in late—"

"Don't sweat it, Susan," Harri answered. "I'll be up, and I'll have my place and Aisha's ready for whatever your family needs."

"Thanks, Harri. I'll text you updates once we're on the road." The signal disconnected.

"Corvus?" Jeremy asked.

Harri shoved her phone back in her jeans pocket. "Don't know yet. There's a possibility it was random vandalism."

"Since when has anything that happened to us been random?" Jeremy raised a blond eyebrow.

"Arthur—"

"I'll put the trace on her phone as a precaution." He crossed to the loft door, but he paused before crossing the threshold and looked at Harri. "Is there any reason I shouldn't tell Tim?"

Her boyfriend had been so busy with the changes to his exoskeleton requested by NASA she wasn't sure he knew what day it was. But she definitely knew she didn't want him jumping back into superhero mode.

However, withholding information to protect him was a sure way to bomb their still-new relationship.

"If he asks," she said.

"Oh, babydoll." Jeremy shook his head. "Even I know Artie will have to go down to the computer lab, and our favorite Gingersnap is not that stupid no matter what half-truth Artie spins."

Jeremy was right, and Harri knew it. She held up her hands in surrender.

"Just emphasize with Tim, I'm only doing this as a precaution."

Arthur nodded sharply. "Yes, ma'am." He disappeared from sight.

Once the door to the stairwell closing echoed back down the hallway, Jeremy turned to her. "How bad is the Kennedys' cabin?"

Harri relayed the list of damages.

Jeremy whistled. "Somebody was definitely being a dick. Do you really think this was Corvus though? Basic vandalism doesn't seem like their style."

"I'm not taking anything at face value." She shook her head and crossed to the refrigerator. "Want a glass of white wine while we wait for our men?"

Jeremy straightened and cocked his head. "You sure you still want to go to the salon's Christmas party tonight?"

"I'm going to continue as if nothing's wrong." Harri retrieved the bottle from the refrigerator and rummaged in the utensil drawer for the opener. "This is probably nothing more than extra people at the table for Christmas dinner."

She crossed her toes and prayed she was right.

CHAPTER 10

Aisha couldn't say her feet were killing her like so many other pregnant women as they waited in line with Devon for Mister Spectacular's autograph. No, she was having a harder time staying on the floor from the third trimester fatigue that plagued her. She spotted a soda machine nearby.

She brought Rey's hand to her lips. "I'm going to get a Coke."

He frowned at her. "You shouldn't be drinking caffeine—"

"Don't. Start." She waggled the index finger of her free hand at him. "I haven't had real coffee in months. One Coke isn't going to kill me or the baby."

Jada and Devon giggled.

The father standing behind them leaned forward. "Dude, haven't you learned from the first two kids? As long as she's not eating powdered detergent, keep your trap shut while the missus is pregnant."

Hiding her own smile, Aisha released Rey's hand, unhooked the burgundy velvet rope used for crowd control from its silver stand, and slipped past before sliding the hook back in place. Jada and Devon joined in picking on Rey, pretending he was their dad, as Aisha headed for the soda machine.

She pulled a bill from the pocket of her phone case and inserted it into the slot. Root beer or Sprite would be a better choice, but other than the one mocha she drank three months ago, she hadn't touched caffeine since Rey came home. Mainly because he monitored everything she put in her mouth like he was her prison warden.

She sighed as she punched the button for a Coke Classic. Her resentment wasn't Rey's fault. He was genuinely concerned about her and their baby. This child was a miracle. Her doctors said she'd never conceive again after an ectopic pregnancy when she'd been married to Cal resulted in so many complications. Her development of HRSP resulted in damn near total invulnerability. Not only did it mean no drugs during delivery, she and the baby were screwed if something went wrong. There's no way her new doctor could do a C-section even though her ob-gyn was experienced in this type of issue. For someone with Rey's power set, knowing he couldn't do a damn thing in this situation was driving him crazy.

The machine spit out her bottle of Coke, and Aisha twisted off the cap. Watching the line of excited kids and their tolerant parents, part of her questioned if taking on the Ghost Owl mantle after the baby's birth was such a bright idea.

Sure, Mister Spectacular seemed to enjoy the adulation, and the donations for his autograph went to charity. However, she already had her hands full with a brand-new law practice, a husband determined to save their neighborhood, and in a couple of months, the birth of her son. Plus, there was no guarantee she'd keep her powers after she delivered. Scientists still hadn't quite figured out how pregnancy hormones affected female supers or created powers in someone who wasn't previously super like herself.

Aisha took a long drink from her bottle. It had been so long since she'd had a real soft drink the sugar rush felt how she imagined a hit of cocaine would. No doubt she would pay for her treat later. But for now, she was revived enough she could keep her feet on the floor.

Aisha eyed the display in the window of a store a little further down the hallway. The mannequin family were dressed for the holidays. Most of the clothing was too warm for Canyon Pointe. Hell, the coats were too much for Atlanta. But underneath the baby mannequin's ski coat was the cutest t-shirt, featuring a cartoon reindeer. In her mind, she pictured dressing her own baby next Christmas.

She glanced over at the line snaking around the huge open space in the courtyard of the mall. It would be some time before Rey and the kids reached Mister Spectacular. Long enough to purchase the t-shirt for her own child.

Aisha caught Rey's attention and pointed at the shop, and he nodded. As long as he knew where she was, he wouldn't tear apart the mall looking for her. He grew up on the streets, homeless after the woman he'd known as his mother was murdered, so he had abandonment and trust issues long before Professor Paranoia kidnapped both him and his twin brother this year.

After taking another long swig of her soda, she screwed the cap back on, stashed the bottle in the special pocket on her canvas tote for that purpose, and headed for the clothing store. The place was neither as full or as empty as she expected with the superhero signing so near to the store's entrance. A perky young saleswoman rushed up breathlessly.

"How can I help you today, ma'am?" She flashed a bright smile.

Ma'am? Aisha tried not to wince or get angry at the young woman. It wasn't her fault she was young enough to be Aisha's daughter. In fact, the clerk was far closer to Rey's age than Aisha was. Exactly the sort of girl Rey should have been dating.

Aisha forced a smile of her own. Dammit. He married her. Hell, he didn't even look at other women. Where was the guilt and insecurity coming from?

Cal. It always came back to her ex-husband.

"There's a t-shirt on the toddler mannequin in the window—"

"Oh, yes! It's been one of our top sellers! What size do you need!"

Harri would have killed the poor girl for her enthusiasm and her loud voice out of sheer principle. Aisha bit her lip to keep from laughing.

"A one-T, please."

"Oh, good! We're out of so-o-o-o-o many of the other sizes!" The clerk beckoned Aisha to follow her. "Like I said! Popular!"

The girl retrieved one of the shirts in the requested size from a nearby display. She held up the shirt and insisted Aisha examine the tiny garment. "Since it's holiday merchandise, you can't return it after New Year's Day."

Spying the price tag, Aisha could understand why the young woman wanted to make sure the customer was satisfied. However, the shirt was too darn cute to pass up. She could already envision her son next Christmas, sitting by the tree and playing with his toys in this little t-shirt.

Right before the baby learned how to fly.

Aisha squished that fear. There was nothing to be done. Their son would most likely have Rey's powers. Her husband was a Mayan demigod after all. And she really needed to stop worrying, or she'd give herself high blood pressure.

She smiled at the clerk. "Looks just fine to me. I definitely want it."

The young woman quickly rang up Aisha's purchase. She folded the t-shirt and slipped it into a handled paper bag stenciled with the store's logo. "Thank you for shopping at—"

A plasma bolt whizzed over the clerk's head and ignited the Christmas sweater on display above the cashwrap.

Chapter 11

The groan of the elevator stopping on the fifth floor and the heavy boots stomping in the hallway warned Harri five seconds before her loft door rolled open. Tim stood in the doorway and glared at her. He must have been working when Arthur got to the computer lab. Dust covered Tim's threadbare jeans and the blue and red plaid flannel shirt over his navy t-shirt though the afternoon light caught glints of metal shavings. She couldn't take him seriously when his silver-threaded red hair stood askew from his sweat, his welding mask and hat, plus his tendency to run his hands through his locks while thinking through a problem. His dark blue eyes were filled with a mix of anger and worry.

"Where's the Kennedy family cabin?" he demanded.

Swallowing her humor, Harri turned to Jeremy. "I should have told Arthur to keep his mouth shut."

Jeremy merely smirked.

"If Corvus is harassing your associate—" Tim started.

"Stop—" Harri thought better of calling her boyfriend a raging paranoid. It wasn't paranoia when a member of the secret, and illegal, black ops organization murdered Tim's family over twenty years ago.

She held up her hands. "Please, just stop for a moment. Susan is aware of all the possibilities. She's bringing her family here to the Lechuza Building as we speak."

"Who's still in town? I'll change and meet them—"

"The Ghost Owl is dead, remember?" Harri and Aisha had to do some fast talking after Professor Paranoia, a Honduran supervillain and worshipper of the Mayan lords of death, had brainwashed Steve. The kid had nearly killed both Tim and Harri. Aisha issued a press release that the original Ghost Owl had died protecting the city from an imposter who had killed Captain Justice and stolen his uniform. In one stroke, they'd killed two superhero identities, but desperate times, yadda, yadda, yadda.

"That doesn't mean—" Tim growled.

"Gingersnap, as much as I love the whole rugged, sweaty, blue-collar look, please tell me you're not wearing that—" Jeremy waved to indicate Tim's tight, worn jeans and perspiration-soaked t-shirt. "—to my company's holiday celebration."

"Corvus is more important than some party!" Tim looked ready to hit something.

"Think about it, honey." Harri crossed her arms. "Simple vandalism isn't Corvus's style. If there are any contacts the FBI hasn't discovered, they would have had a hit team waiting for Susan and her family at the cabin."

"Or rigged it to blow up," Jeremy added.

"Trubble could be issuing orders from prison—" Tim started.

"And I'm at the top of his naughty list," Harri pointed out. She crossed over to him and wrapped her arms around his waist. "Not Susan or her family. If you're right and it is Corvus, this is the safest place for the Kennedys to be." She grinned up at him. "And as much as I love your very masculine smell, you need to take a shower. Leonardo will be here in a couple of hours to pick us up."

Tim frowned down at her as his arms encircled her. "I can drive now, remember?"

She tried not to think about the six months of rehab so he could walk again. He still limped when Canyon Pointe had a cloudburst, the temperatures got below the fifties, or he was simply tired.

"And here I thought no one could out-boss Harri," Jeremy said snidely.

"You're not helping, Jaye," she returned with a faux-cheerful tone.

"That's Lady Jaye to you, girlfriend." Jeremy punctuated his remark with a snap of his fingers.

She ignored Jeremy's queen bitchiness. "Susan's going to text me updates on their trip back—" Sure enough, her phone beeped.

Harri released Tim and pulled the device from her pocket. "Speak of the devil."

She read the message. "The sheriff wrote up the report. A couple of neighbors helped them board up the place. Insurance can't get there until after the holidays, so they're on the way back now."

She looked up at Tim. "Will you please go shower and change?" She waved her phone. "This won't leave my side all night, and you'll know every time the Kennedys stop for gas or a pee break.

"Fine," Tim spat. He turned and stomped back towards the elevator.

Once the groaning of the antique elevator indicated it was descending, Jeremy said, "The enforced rest didn't do him any good."

"Tell me about it," Harri grumbled. She eyed Jeremy. "I half-expected him to accuse me of killing off the Ghost Owl persona on purpose."

Jeremy harrumphed. "It was better than the authorities jailing Gingersnap for vigilantism. You know the courts wouldn't cut him any slack even though you proved Seismic Shit was the real murderer." He rose from his stool. "Now, will you please let me do something with that hair of yours, Harriet? I can't take you to my salon's party looking like—"

"Looking like what?" she snapped.

"The Ghost Owl's mother." A wicked grin split his face.

"Who told you about—" Harri grimaced. She'd relented on letting Jeremy do something about her own gray hairs after one of the gals at Tim's rehab thought she was his mother. "I'm going to kill Aisha when she gets home."

Chapter 12

⸺ ◆ ⬥ ◆ ⸺

Screams came from shoppers inside the store as well as out in the mall courtyard where the charity signing was happening. Aisha had to give the perky clerk credit for keeping her head. The girl yanked a fire extinguisher from behind the cashwrap. White fog shot from the nozzle. The charred remains of the sweater and some Christmas decorations were the only immediate damage from the plasma bolt.

Another clerk smacked the button to close the store's gates. A few more shoppers ducked inside in their attempt to escape whatever was happening as the gates lowered. Another plasma bolt hit one of the picture windows framing the main entrance of the store. The glass cracked from the intense heat, but the pane didn't break.

Aisha cursed silently to herself. She should have darted out into the main part of the mall while she had the chance, but everything happened so fast. Maybe if she stalled, let everyone inside the store escape . . .

A third clerk herded shoppers toward the back of the store. The young lady who had waited on Aisha charged from behind the cashwrap, the extinguisher still in her hand.

"Come on, ma'am." The clerk wrapped her free arm around Aisha's left elbow. "We need to evacuate." She tugged Aisha in the direction the rest of the people were fleeing.

"But my husband—" Aisha tried to gently pull free, but the clerk had a good grip on her. If she pulled any harder, she'd hurt the young lady. "My kids—"

"We can't help them, ma'am." The clerk tugged on Aisha's arm again. "You need to think about the little one with you. Mister Spectacular will protect your family and everyone else's."

Dammit! Aisha gritted her teeth. *What is it about pregnancy that everyone else went nuts? Thought she was a total invalid just because she was lugging another person around inside of her body.*

Nothing in the law specialty gossip mill said Mister Spectacular was a moron or incompetent. But there had to be a couple hundred people waiting to see him, and more than one source of the plasma bolts. And from the angle where she stood, she could count three bodies on the ceramic floor tiles. However, she had no idea if they were alive or dead.

Even worse, she couldn't see Rey and the kids from here.

The other clerk who had closed the gates latched onto Aisha's right elbow. If she shook them off, she'd reveal herself before she even got her superhero career off the ground. She didn't have any choice but to let the two employees lead her to the back of the store.

They passed through the storage room and entered the service corridor before the supervillain alarm pierced the air. The hallway was so crowded Aisha wrapped her arms around her protruding abdomen.

For the first time, real fear hit her. Her skin may be invulnerable, but that didn't mean her baby couldn't be trampled to death if the crowd of shoppers and employees panicked. If it weren't for the hold the clerks had on her elbows, she would be floating to the ceiling about now. She gritted her teeth, attempting to get her emotions under control.

More people poured into the corridor from other stores. Some crying, some injured. Ahead, a security guard stood in an alcove, motioning with his flashlight and calling out for people to keep moving. Another woman stopped next to him and begged for help. With so many people in the corridor making noise, Aisha only caught something about her children.

"Ma'am, there isn't anything you or I can do," the guard said. "SWAT's on their way. The best thing you can do for your kids is get out of the way so the professionals can do their job."

Despite the man's rude rebuke, an idea sparked in Aisha's brain. "You two ladies, go ahead. I see a friend of mine, and it looks like she's in the same trouble."

"We can't leave you," the first clerk protested.

"My friend's the lady with the security guard." Aisha pointed at them and lowered her voice. "If Karen panics in here, so will everyone else. I promise we'll be right behind you."

The two young women released her and exchanged glances as they walked.

The second clerk shrugged. "If you can help—"

"But you'd better be right behind us." The first clerk glared at Aisha.

"I promise." Aisha crossed her heart.

"Good luck." The second clerk waved before they were swallowed by the mass of humans flowing down the corridor.

"Karen! There you are!" This time, Aisha latched onto the distraught woman's arm.

"Ladies, you need to evacuate!" The security guard was losing his patience, but from the sheen of sweat on his forehead, it had more to do with his own fear rather than the shopper's panic.

"What?" The lady looked up at Aisha in shock. "Who—"

Aisha used a little bit of her strength and hustled the woman further down the hall, away from the guard. She leaned close to the woman's ear. "I'm here to help. Did you get a good look at who attacked the shoppers in the main hall of the mall?"

Agony swept over the woman's face. Her dark brown eyes filled with tears. "My kids were in line for Mister Spectacular's signing. I stepped away for a moment to answer my husband's phone call, and they burst in through the entrance on the other side of the courtyard."

"The perps?" Aisha hissed. Another alcove appeared, she dragged the woman into the tiny shelter while the flood of humans rolled past them.

"They were dressed like Santa's elves." The woman's throat bobbed as she clutched her Louis Vuitton purse to her chest. "You know, the red and white striped shirts, green shorts with suspenders and tights, but they all had masks on. All except one who seemed to be the leader. He was dressed in orange and green. It looked like an opposite of Mister Spectacular's costume."

For someone on the verge of panic, she was remarkably observant. But then, both the heroes and the villains wanted all attention on them. Sometimes, for the same reason.

"Thank you." Aisha smiled at her.

The woman glanced at Aisha's hand still holding her bicep before she whispered, "Do you have mind powers in addition to strength?"

"What?" Aisha released the other woman. "I don't have either."

"I won't say anything." The woman smiled despite her glistening eyes. "I'm just glad one of you is here. My last name is Hamilton. My daughters are Tonya and Katelyn."

"What's your first name?" Aisha asked.

The woman appeared confused. "Karen."

Aisha couldn't help it. She laughed. "I'm so sorry. I was just throwing out a name."

"Sure." It was obvious the woman didn't believe a word she said.

"The guard is right though." Aisha gestured at the other evacuees. "It's safer for everyone if you get out of here. We don't want to give the supervillain more hostages."

Karen nodded and merged with the rest of the shoppers. Her black hair disappeared in the rushing crowd.

Aisha gritted her teeth. Rey would stay with the kids, but she prayed Steve wouldn't do something stupid in the meantime. Now, she just needed to figure out how to avoid the guards, find a disguise, and re-enter the mall without getting caught.

Okay, maybe she didn't have to worry only about Steve being stupid.

CHAPTER 13

When Harri walked into the ballroom of the Grand Royale Hotel with Tim, Jeremy, and Leonardo, the swirl of glitter, color, and perfume made her head swim. Jeremy's salon party was not only for his employees, but his clientele as well. That meant it was the place to see and be seen by Canyon Pointe's LGBT community, certain supers, and society matrons. While Harri hated most of the society bitches with a passion, Jeremy's queen friends and some of the supers were a blast to party with.

The ballroom fitted the swanky attendees. Rich burgundy carpet covered the perimeter with a hardwood dance floor in the middle. When the hotel was restored ten years ago, the owners managed to find the same gold and burgundy wallpaper that had decorated the place when it was built at the height of the mining boom over a century ago. The chairs and tables were covered with gold fabric to hide the fact they were standard hotel conference portables.

As usual, Harri wore the black tuxedo Jeremy designed for her. This year, her tie and handkerchief were hot pink. Tim wore the same navy suit he'd worn the first time she and Aisha looked at the Lechuza Building. Leonardo wore a similar black tuxedo as Harri, but a black bowtie with a gold lace overlay adorned his throat. The same gold lace that formed the bodice and overlaid the black skirt of Jeremy's evening dress.

Tonight, Jeremy didn't bother with a wig. His makeup was as sedate and as impeccable as the cosmetics he applied to Harri's face. Aisha often said God accidentally installed Harri's software in Jeremy and vice versa until Harri and Jeremy had moved into the Franklins' home when they were teens.

The one time Betty overheard Aisha's comment, she responded that

God didn't make mistakes, which sent Jeremy running to the room he shared with Aisha's brother Martin, crying. Harri and Aisha heard Jeremy wail if God didn't make mistakes Betty and Marvin would have been his and Harri's parents. Aisha never said the software thing again.

Harri's phone beeped, and she pulled it out of her inside jacket pocket. She looked up at Tim. "The Kennedy clan is making their first pit stop before they get on the interstate. No problems so far."

He nodded absently, his eyes scanning the crowd. "Good. The mountain road would have been the most opportune place for a night ambush."

"Would you please stop?" she whispered. "You're acting like a combat vet with PTSD."

He looked down at her. "After the last seven months, you really expect me not to be on my guard?"

She sighed. "I hoped with the crows behind bars you'd be able to enjoy yourself a little."

"Of course, I can enjoy—" Tim froze like a purebred pointer.

"What?" She pivoted to find whatever spooked him, but nothing seemed out of the ordinary, other than Judge Inunza laughing a little too loud at whatever Felicity Wilcox had said to him and his wife Carol. She turned back to Tim. "What did you see?"

"Someone I used to know." Concern knitted his brows into a series of deep lines. "Or maybe I am stressed enough to be imagining things."

His forehead smoothed, and his charming, sexy smile flashed across his face. "You are totally right. I need to learn how to have fun again. Want to teach me?"

Harri chuckled despite herself. However, a little worry nagged beneath her psyche. Tim may jump at shadows, but those shadows were usually dangerous, if not deadly.

"Of course," she replied cheerfully. "Let's get some food first, then we'll teach these kids how to cut a rug."

⁂

One of the great things about Jeremy's Christmas parties was that buffet and dining tables were stationed around the carpeted perimeter of the ballroom. The arrangement let people circulate through the room and chat, rather than being stuck at a more formal dinner with people you didn't particularly like. Harri hated the small talk schtick, too, so she darted from group to group with the minimum chatter as she made her way to the dessert table.

Tim was her proverbial shadow for the trip. The surprise and shock on some of the old biddies' faces were worth it when they realized who her date was. They arrived at the dessert table right behind Judge Inunza and Carol.

"Harri!" The judge pumped her hand. "How's it going?"

"Just fine, sir." She exchanged hugs with Carol. "Tim, this is Judge Pablo Inunza and Carol Inunza. Folks, this is Tim Canyon."

The judge held out his hand to Tim. "You probably don't remember me—"

"That you were my grandfather's caddy when I was a child, or that you were Judge Shepard's staff attorney when I was arraigned for my wife and son's murders?"

Harri wanted to stomp on Tim's foot, but the judge's smile merely turned wry.

"You must admit, Mr. Canyon, in your case the system worked exactly as it was designed."

"There's a big difference between being acquitted and being declared innocent," Tim said. His expression was that unreadable one, which meant he was holding in some strong emotion.

"And yet, Harri here did prove your innocence by catching the real culprit," the judge responded.

"Carol," Harri interjected. "Why don't we get some dessert while these two rehash ancient history?"

"Ancient?" the judge and Tim said at the same time.

"Ancient," Carol said with a smirk. She looped her left arm around

Harri's right. "And I like the way you think, counselor. Chocolate first at these shindigs."

Once the two women had their plates loaded with double chocolate cheesecake and a sampling of the liquor-filled truffles, they grabbed an empty nearby table.

"So, Tim Canyon, huh?" Carol said before she forked a bite of cheesecake into her mouth. The ballroom chandeliers highlighted her short salt, pepper, and fuchsia hair.

But then, Carol Inunza had always marched to the beat of her own drum. She'd successfully sued her employer for ethnic bias in Hermanville over her colorful pantsuits. Everyone in Canyon Point had been surprised she attracted the attention of the by-the-book Pablo Inunza.

"And?" Harri prompted.

"It's good to see you getting over Eddie finally." Carol smiled.

Harri groaned. "Is that really what the rumor mill is saying about us?"

"Does it matter to either of you what the gossip mongers are pitching?" Carol shook her head and gestured at the photographer in the corner taking a picture of the judge and Tim. "However, it will be all over the society section in tomorrow morning's edition of the paper."

"Does anyone read newsprint anymore?" Harri answered with a grin of her own.

Carol leaned closer. "Only the ancient assholes who already hate our guts for shaking up their system."

"Now, what are you two girls whispering about?" Felicity Wilcox slid into a seat at their table. Her bright red dress made tinkling noises from the zillions of crystals decorating it. Matching lipstick covered her artificially plumped lips. The colors amplified the minute plastic surgery scars on her face and the thinning of her white hair instead of hiding them.

Speaking of ancient assholes. Harri fixed her society smile on her face. It wasn't hard to miss that Carol did the same.

"Carol was asking me where Jeremy ordered the cheesecake."

"Uh-huh." Thanks to Felicity's botox treatments, her face barely moved, but there definitely was a malicious gleam in her eyes. "It's nice to see you brought a male escort to this year's party, Harri."

She could feel her blood pressure rise. Playing Felicity's stupid game wasn't smart, but Harri kind of wished she was wearing one of the Ghost Owl suits so she could Tase the bitch.

"Harri, you didn't say you were going to pay me." Tim pulled out the chair between Harri and Felicity while the judge sat next to Carol.

Tim's plate was loaded with hors d'oeuvres, mainly of the vegetable variety. "Those truffles look delicious." He picked one off of Harri's plate and popped it into his mouth. With a groan, he rolled his eyes. "So that's what I haven't been able to afford all these years." He took another one. "Maybe I should stick my vegetables in a Ziplock and eat them for lunch tomorrow. These are to die for!"

He was deliberately being crass. On one hand, Harri didn't blame him after Felicity's insult. On the other, this behavior wasn't going to help with rehabilitating his image.

Oh, god. Now she was thinking exactly like Aisha would.

"Why don't I get us some champagne?" Harri started to rise.

"Wait!" Tim pressed her thigh with his right hand and waved excitedly at the photographer with his left. "We need a picture first. Right, Felicity?" He wrapped his left arm around Felicity.

Before Felicity could object, the flashbulb went off in Harri's eyes. By the time, the spots on her retinas faded, the society matron was gone.

"Was that necessary?" Harri hissed under her breath.

"If I'm going to be on the front page of the society section again, it'll be on my terms." His calmness was a facade, and they both knew it.

"You might want to listen to your attorney, Mr. Canyon," Carol said softly. "There's a time to tweak the noses of the powers-that-be, and there are times when you need to let things lie."

A rueful expression crossed Tim's face. "You're right, Mrs. Inunza. I apologize to you and your husband for my behavior." He turned to Harri. "I'm definitely sorry for embarrassing you." He raised her hand to his lips and kissed the back of it.

A little self-deprecating laugh escaped her throat. "I think I'm more worried that you're acting like me."

"Aw, come on." Tim gave her an impish grin. "It's not like I Tased her."

CHAPTER 14

"Aisha!"

She looked over her shoulder. Both of her brothers-in-law towered over most of the crowd still flooding the corridor. She stepped into another alcove that held the back door to another mall shop and waited for the men to catch up.

"Are you all right?" Steve said at the same time Eric said, "Where are Jada and Devon?"

"I'm fine." She grimaced. "Rey and the kids are trapped with the rest of the fans inside the courtyard where Mister Spectacular was signing autographs. Steve, cover for me."

He angled his body so no one could see her wrench the latch and break the lock.

"What about the authorities?" Eric muttered.

"By the time, they get here only God knows what could happen." She looked up at him. "You need to get to safety."

"Are my children safe?" Eric growled. "You're the one who shouldn't be here. Not with your own baby on the way."

This wasn't worth arguing about with him. Aisha sucked in a breath and slipped into the dark storeroom. Despite Eric's irritation, he followed her inside. With a quick check of the thinning crowd, Steve followed.

"What's the plan?" Steve asked.

"We need disguises to deal with the supervillain and his goons," Aisha said as she flipped on the light switch. Last thing she needed was Eric tripping over something in the dark.

"Didn't you bring your supersuit?" Steve murmured.

Aisha looked down at her protruding stomach and back at Steve. "Sweetie, that suit fitting was two trimesters ago."

"Wait a minute." Eric stared at Steve and her like they were both crazy. "You're going into the actual superhero business? After everything that happened to Rey?"

"This isn't the time to discuss my career choices." Aisha scowled at him. "One of the witnesses said the supervillain's minions were dressed like the mall's elves and the villain was dressed in an orange and green costume." She examined the labels of the boxes on the storage shelves. Crap, they all seemed to be ornaments, wreaths, and lights. With her luck, she'd broken into a Christmas supply shop.

Steve frowned. "The Orange King maybe? Though he's not one of Mister Spectacular's archnemeses, and he usually haunts Florida."

"Maybe he's moving north," Eric said. "Everyone and their mother are moving to Atlanta these days. Just like Portland."

Aisha turned to face him. "Do you know where the mall's Santa and elves change clothes?"

"Are you kidding me?" Eric stared at her in disbelief. "I've never worked here!"

"It's got to be near the North Pole." Steve winced as he realized how that sounded. "I mean, near the mall's photos with Santa set-up."

"The problem is the service corridors will be flooded with superheroes and police any second," Eric said.

"No." Aisha shook her head. "They'll bring in a negotiator first."

"Then shouldn't we let this negotiator do their job?" Steve asked.

"Normally, I'd say yes." Aisha shook her head again. "But something doesn't smell right about this."

"What do you mean?" Eric said.

"Hostages aren't the Orange King's style, and someone was shooting plasma bolts." Aisha crossed to the door into the store. "Plasma blasts aren't in his power set." She twisted the knob, eased the door open a couple of inches, and peered into the store. Nobody appeared to be inside, and the main doors were glass, closed and probably locked. The store's lights were out, but the main hallway's halogens shone through the windows.

"Maybe the Orange King invented a weapon to throw people off," Eric muttered. "Or maybe it's one of Mister Spectacular's regular nemeses."

"Mister Spectacular doesn't have a nemesis with plasma powers," Steve whispered.

"Do you have the whole NSB registry memorized?" Eric hissed.

"Almost," Steve replied.

Great. She was attempting to sneak through a mall at Christmas with a supervillain and their minions on the loose and two brothers-in-law doing an Abbot and Costello routine. Maybe she was better off doing this by herself.

On the other hand, she had never tried to rescue civilians before now. This was a whole lot different than taking on Steve or Rey. They may have been mind-controlled by Professor Paranoia, but both incidents had been in fairly isolated areas. Not smack dab in the middle of a major city.

"We're still in the cross hallway from the courtyard." Irritation prickled along Aisha's skin. "We'd have to get to one of the stores across the way and break into it without being seen by the supervillain and the minions."

Behind her, paper rattled. "One of the anchor stores is to our right, correct?" Steve murmured.

"Yeah." Aisha looked over her shoulder. Steve had a brochure.

He tapped the shiny page. "There's a hallway to the public restrooms right before the main entrance to the anchor." He looked up at her. "If Lenox Square is like other malls, there's a passage to the service corridor for that side of the mall."

"Where did you get that?" she asked.

Steve gestured at the stack of brochures on what was obviously the store manager's desk.

Aisha rolled her eyes.

"What about the bad guys?" Eric waved at the door they came through.

"We need to move faster than them," Aisha said. She crept closer to the front windows. Luckily, there were floor to ceiling posters hanging in the window displays. She stayed behind shelves and fake trees as best as she could, which was a little difficult while hauling around a person who kept wanting to kick her liver into the next state. The real problem was opening those glass doors without alerting the bad guys. When she reached the front of the store, she breathed a little sigh of relief. The doors had twist knobs for the deadbolts instead of needing a key on the inside of the store.

"We need to move fast," Steve commented. "I'll carry you." He reached for Eric who jumped back.

"You are not carrying me, man!" Eric protested.

"Keep it down, you guys," Aisha hissed. "And yes, he is unless you evacuate with the rest of the civilians. Or would you prefer I carry you?"

Eric make a face. "Fine. Steve can carry me."

Aisha tried not to laugh at the comical sight of one brother-in-law in the other's arms. She knelt before the door and prayed no one looked in their direction as she twisted the knob.

Thank goodness, the staff kept the lock well lubricated. She rose and yanked the door open. Steve darted through with Eric in his arms and raced toward the anchor store.

Aisha clambered to her feet and ran after the guys. She just turned down the corridor to the public restrooms when a plasma bolt hit the wall behind her.

CHAPTER 15

Harri breathed a little sigh of relief an hour later. Tim kept his promise and behaved himself impeccably. While she agreed with Carol about tweaking noses at the right time and place, Jeremy's party was not it. There obviously was some bad blood between Tim and Felicity, but was it personal, or was there a Canyon-Wilcox family feud of which she was unaware? Either way, this party wasn't the time to grill Tim about it. She'd save it for the ride home.

Other than Felicity's snippiness, everyone else used their society manners. There was a bit of teasing Tim about coming back to Canyon Pointe after all the rumors that he'd been living on a tropical island, but nothing to the level of what she feared. Harri finally felt comfortable enough to leave him to get another glass of wine. Waiting in line, she was talking with Ultramegaperson and two of the granddaughters of the Canyon Pointe Copperheads' owner when her phone buzzed.

"Excuse me a moment." Harri smiled at the other guests before she strolled away and pulled her phone from her inside jacket pocket. She thumbed the notice of a text from Arthur and read the message.

Sry to bother u. Supervillain hostage sit in ATL.

Crap. Harri tapped the headlines icon. Sure enough, an unknown supervillain had taken hostages in Lenox Square Mall. Fear raced through her blood. Maybe she should have listened to Tim about Susan and her family.

Harri flipped through the rest of her texts. Nope, Susan and her family were fine. Their associate had her nephew texting their progress every half hour. The kid added the name of a different superhero client to the end of each text to confirm it was legit.

Another text popped up. This one was from Betty.

Have you heard from Aisha or Rey? I can't reach them.

Double crap. Betty was smart. No one got away with anything in her home when Harri, Jeremy, and Aisha were kids. Betty was also fiercely protective of those people she considered her family. Her text was her way of letting Harri know Aisha and Rey were in the middle of the mall mess.

Surely, they wouldn't do anything stupid before they officially registered, or in Rey's case, re-registered. But Steve was with them, and the twins together with Aisha always resulted in mayhem. And just like the chaos in Japan, there wasn't a damn thing Harri could do. Whatever was going down at the Lenox Square Mall would be over by the time she could book a flight.

Hell, not even Ultramegaperson could fly halfway across the country to reach Atlanta in time to stop Aisha and the twins from doing—well, whatever Harri was sure they were doing.

"Have you seen the news?" Tim murmured in her ear.

It was all she could do not to jump.

"Yeah," she said. "I also got texts from Arthur and Betty."

"Do we need to leave?"

As much as she wanted to, there wasn't a damn thing either of them could do to help. And if Aisha and the guys were in the middle of that mess, texting Aisha this minute could get someone killed. However, she was more worried about the glint in Tim's eyes. The one that said he was about to jump into superhero mode.

"What exactly are you planning to do, Mr. Canyon?" She looked up at him.

He opened his mouth and apparently realized how stupid whatever he was about to say would be. "Guess there isn't much we can do in this case, is there?"

"Not this time." Harri glanced at the article on her phone again. "Not unless you suddenly developed the ability to teleport."

Tim pursed his lips before he said, "That's a project I'll set Francisco on."

Harri sighed. It would be hard to enjoy herself at Jeremy's party, knowing her partner was in danger. "We can make out apologies and call a taxi."

He nodded. "You do the first, and I'll get us a ride."

As she watched Tim head for the exit, a throaty voice said, "Something wrong, Harri, darling?"

Ultramegaperson stepped closer. Their rainbow-colored tresses were definitely Leo's work, as much as the gown in the super's trademark silver and purple was Jeremy's. However, their makeup was a take on their usual mask. Since Jeremy had been doing Harri's prior to the party, either Ultramegaperson had one hell of a makeup artist or was one themself.

"I know I'm not a Canyon Pointe regular, but if there's something I can do to help?"

Harri forced a polite smile. "I don't think there's a thing any of us can do from here. My law partner's in Atlanta with her family for the holidays, and a news report just popped up that there's a supervillain incident involving hostages at Lenox Square Mall."

Ultramegaperson's eyes narrowed. "Mister Spectacular has his annual signing for charity at that mall."

A chill ran through Harri. Aisha's nephew Devon was obsessed with meeting superheroes and obtaining their autographs. If Devon had finagled a trip to the mall to get Mister Spectacular's autograph, no wonder Betty was worried.

"Aisha Franklin never struck me as the type to go gaga over a super," Ultramegaperson said.

"Not her, but she'd do anything for her nephew." The chill inside

Harri turned to ice. Whatever denial she held in her heart died from the frozen feeling filling her.

"I'll make some phone calls to friends. See if I can find out what's going on." Ultramegaperson pulled their phone from inside the bosom of their dress. "What's your cell number, darling?"

Harri hesitated for a split second, only because she was used to being a city attorney and trying to collect money from supers for damages to infrastructure from their battles. Including Ultramegaperson.

But they appeared to genuinely want to help in this situation.

"It's easier if I just enter it." Harri held out her hand.

Ultramegaperson gave her the phone and grinned. "You were worried I'd leave you on top of the Del Oro Bank Building?"

Harri punched in her number and grinned back. "It's been threatened before." She returned the phone. "Thank you. I really appreciate this."

"Oh, I'm being totally self-serving, darling. I planned on making an appointment with Winters & Franklin after the holidays. I don't want to see you lose your partner either." Ultramegaperson winked at her as they sauntered off, the phone raised to their ear.

The idea of a superhero of Ultramegaperson's stature should have had Harri salivating, but it didn't make a dent in the ball of ice her gut had become.

She hurried over to Jeremy who was speaking with Mayor Benevides and the new police chief Lloyd Harrison. "Excuse me, gentlemen. I just wanted to extend my thanks to our host before I call it a night."

"Excuse me, gentlemen." Jeremy looped his arm around Harri's and guided her away from the other guests. The gracious smile on his face didn't reach his eyes. They paused near the exit.

"What's happened?" Jeremy murmured.

"Hostage situation in Atlanta." Harri grimaced. "Guess who's in the middle of it."

"Shit." Jeremy shook his head. "There's nothing you can do from here. Are you planning to fly there? The authorities and Mister Spectacular will have it wrapped up before the plane gets past Texas."

"From the sound of things on the news app, he's one of the hostages." She patted Jeremy's hand. "Go and have a good time at your party. Ultramegaperson's making some calls for me. You know me. I'll worry regardless. I didn't want to bring down the mood."

"Text me when you have some news whether it's Aisha or Susan." Jeremy scanned the other guests. "Where's Gingersnap?"

"Already getting us a ride. It was a lovely party as always." Harri reached up and pecked him on the cheek. "See you at Christmas dinner."

"Be careful." Jeremy hugged her, and she returned his tight hold.

"Always."

Jeremy harrumphed under his breath as Harri darted out of the ballroom. She was rather glad she wore the tux rather than an evening gown. It was definitely easier to move in trousers. From the way her breath turned to steam when she exited the hotel, the temperature had dropped faster than the meteorologist on Action 12! News had estimated.

Tim was the only person by the cab stand besides one of the doormen. Harri rushed over to the taxi. The doorman helped her inside while Tim slid into the back seat from the opposite door.

"How drunk are you tonight, Ms. Winters?"

She watched the driver's reflection in the rearview mirror as the taxi rolled to the end of the hotel's drive. He seemed vaguely familiar. "Pardon me?"

"You don't remember me?" Their driver chuckled as he turned right onto Commerce Avenue. "Well, you did have more than one margarita the night I picked up you and the other guy from La Churro's last summer."

"He's right," Tim added. "You were pretty drunk the night after Grace was born."

She examined the driver's picture and name. "Dopinder? Weren't you the guy who moved here from New York to get away from the supers scene?"

"You remember!" he said cheerfully as he made another right turn and headed toward the Canyon Block.

"You asked me for Captain Justice's autograph."

Dopinder's face fell. "Yeah, my kids were heartbroken when he died." He cleared his throat. "I hope you and CJ made up before . . ."

Harri wasn't sure what to say. That was right around the time Rey disappeared and a brainwashed Steve replaced him, so she'd been arguing with both men the week of Grace's birth. She certainly couldn't tell their driver the truth that Rey was still alive though. Dopinder seemed like a sweet man, and a kindness would be better. Maybe she was learning something from Aisha's style of practicing law after all.

"Yes, we did," Harri said. "And I must thank you, Dopinder. That night in your taxi, you pointed out people often make assumptions about each other. Because of your wise words, I made up with someone I care about before he was lost."

Their driver was quiet for a several blocks before he murmured, "I'm glad you found peace with your friend."

"If you have a moment to wait after you drop us off, I have some signed things for your children, including some Captain Justice merchandise." She smiled as Dopinder flashed a surprised look at her via the rearview mirror. "You said they were collectors, right?"

"You don't have to do that, Ms. Winters," he protested. "Not with your personal keepsakes."

"Look at it this way," she said. "It's superhero stuff you don't have to buy, and it will make you the coolest dad ever."

"How do I know you're not just cleaning out your closets?" he said sourly.

Harri laughed despite her fear for Aisha and her family. "You got me. My new boyfriend actually wants some space now that he's moved in with me." She reached over and clasped Tim's hand.

Dopinder laughed, too. "Now that I do understand."

A few minutes later, Tim paid their taxi driver while Harri ran inside her office and loaded two shopping bags with anything she thought a kid might like from her client product sample stash. T-shirts, coloring books, comics. Cobblestone's action figure. Nix's glittery nail polish kit. A remote controlled motorcycle based on Sparx's real one. Sourpuss's smart phone cover. And of course, the rare signed Captain Justice Memorial calendar.

She raced back out to the garage where the men waited.

Dopinder stared at the two very full bags. "That's very generous, but I can't possibly—"

"Yes, you can." She stalked around to the front passenger door of the cab.

Tim chuckled. "I wouldn't argue with her. You aren't going to win this one."

Harri set down one bag and yanked the door open. "You'll be the best dad. Ever." She shoved the bags onto the passenger seat and slammed the door shut. "Happy Holidays!"

Dopinder shook his head while she rounded the front of his vehicle. He produced a few business cards and held them out his open window. "If you or any of your clients need a discreet ride, I'd be happy to help."

She took the cards. "Do you have an unmarked minivan?"

He frowned. "How did you know?"

"Because she's had to use our building manager's to pick up clients before," Tim said.

"And it's very thoughtful for you to volunteer when you've been trying to get away from superhero culture," Harri added.

Dopinder shook his head again. "Good evening, ma'am. Sir." The taxi rolled out of the garage's exit.

"I'm going downstairs to check on Arthur," Tim said as they walked into the building.

"All right." Thankfully, she had worn her stylish black boots, so she could match his stride without running. "I'll come with you."

He paused in front of the elevator. "Why don't you go upstairs and make sure everything's ready for the Kennedys? They'll be here in a few hours."

Harri's phone beeped.

"That's probably them with an update," Tim said. He tilted her chin and gave her a delicate kiss full of promise. "I'll be up soon."

"You'd better be," Harri warned.

Tim headed toward the staircase to the basement. It was separate from the main staircase for the other floors because it led to what had been a fallout shelter beneath the Lechuza building. A fallout shelter that was the hideout of Tim's alter ego, Jatz'om Kuh, the Ghost Owl.

She couldn't miss the way he limped either. The high front with its chillier than usual air was affecting his joints and freshly healed bones. He should have taken the elevator, but if she so much as mentioned it, he would have said he needed the exercise. Only she would have fallen in love with a man just as obsessive and stubborn as she was.

Harri jabbed the elevator button. The building's antique lift groaned as it eased down to the first floor. She opened the gates and entered.

On the ride up, she checked her phone. This text was from Qiang, a list of gifts for her son that she wanted to purchase. As the elevator wheezed past the fourth floor, raucous laughter echoed down the hall. It meant Connor had arrived, and the Esperanza boys were doing their best to keep their guest occupied. Harri hoped they weren't keeping Grace up, but no doubt Miguel or Patty would quiet the boys at the baby's bedtime.

Harri check the hour as the elevated halted on her floor. It was earlier than she thought. She shoved the elevator gates shut and headed for her loft door. As much as a glass of wine would be nice, she didn't want to fall asleep before the Kennedys arrived. Plus, she needed to call Betty and find out what was happing in Atlanta. She punched in the code for her loft and rolled the door open.

The lights were already on, and a gorgeous brunette perched on one of the IKEA pine stools at Harri's kitchen island. The bottle of red wine Harri had been saving for Christmas Eve with Tim sat open next to the stranger. Part of its contents rested in one of Harri's wine glasses.

"Hi, Harri." The woman saluted her with the wine glass, the red liquid inside shifting with the motion. "I hope you don't mind me making myself comfortable in your loft since Aisha and the twins aren't home."

Comfortable isn't what Harri would have called the tight, black, and very short dress or the four-inch heels the woman wore. In fact, she seemed vaguely familiar. But as long as she wasn't making a threatening move, Harri would play along.

"Who are you, why are you here, and how did you get into this building?"

The woman shrugged and sipped the wine. "Let's just say I have a talent for getting into places other people don't want me. I'm here to hire you."

"You couldn't call during normal business hours?"

The woman sighed. "It's not that simple. I would like you to arrange for me to see my family for the holiday."

"And you didn't break into their place because . . ."

"Because this needs to be done on neutral territory, and your building would be the best place."

Harri cocked her head. "Are you insane? I've got my own family celebration to deal with. Besides, you still haven't told me who you are."

"I'm Monica Reinhold."

Harri would have sworn her heart stopped beating. Monica Reinhold, AKA the infamous supervillain Miss Purrception.

Even worse, Tim's ex-girlfriend.

CHAPTER 16

Aisha ran, or rather jogged, down the short hallway. In addition to the two public restrooms, there were two other doors. Steve had put down Eric and broken into the first one.

Crap. A supply closet.

Adrenaline coursed through her as she wrenched the knob of the other door. The lock snapped, and she yanked the door open. A service corridor, and it was empty. She shoved Eric though the doorway. Steve ripped off the knob to the supply closet and darted into the corridor. She eased the door shut while Steve molded the metal into a wedge shape. He knelt and jammed it into the narrow space between the door and the floor tile.

Aisha wanted to breathe a sigh of relief, but her feet left the floor, and she drifted toward the ceiling.

Eric looked up at her. "The Thanksgiving parade was last month."

"I wouldn't make jokes if I were you," Steve murmured as he stood. "Or did you already forget she has superstrength?"

Aisha ignored Eric's jibe, closed her eyes, and focused on her breathing exercises. Who knew Lamaze techniques would be useful for landing? When her soles touched the floor, she opened her eyes.

Noises came from the public hallway they'd just left. She gestured for the guys to follow, and she set off at a brisk pace. Once the service corridor made a ninety-degree turn and she couldn't detect the supervillain minions with her HRSP-enhanced hearing, she figured it was safe enough to talk again.

"Steve, you still have that map?" she asked.

"Yep." He produced the brochure and handed it over to her.

"It's not going to show the service areas," Eric protested.

"No, but the changing area has to be near the North Pole." Aisha checked the names and numbers of the stores as they passed and compared them to the layout on the brochure.

"Wait a minute." Eric held out his hand for the brochure, and she gave it to him. "The North Pole is over here." He turned to orient himself while he twisted the map and examined it. "Santa and the elves would need someplace to duck out quickly." He drew a line between the section for meeting Santa and the closest anchor store. "The management office is on the opposite side of the mall. Too far for a quick disappearing act. I bet we'll find Santa's changing room inside Macy's."

"Great. Let's go." Aisha headed back in their original direction.

"Wait." Eric grabbed her arm. "Let me go first."

"What?" She cocked her head. Had he lost his damn mind?

"Look, I know you're perfectly capable, but we all need to protect your baby." He looked so damn sweet and serious it was hard to be angry with him, but she couldn't stop the wave of exasperation.

Aisha shook her head. "Eric, what would LaShun tell you right now?"

"This is different," he snapped.

"Yeah, it is." Aisha patted his upper arm. "Those plasma bolts may burn off my clothes, but they will hurt or kill you."

He looked at Steve, obviously figuring Rey's brother would back him up.

Steve raised his hands, palms outward and fingers spread. "Dude, she beat me over the head with a tree trunk. Do you really think I'm going to take your side?"

Thankfully, the supervillain alarm cut off. The noise had been adding to the headache the guys' arguing had started.

Aisha strode down the hallway, thankful Eric kept any other objections to himself. A couple of minutes later they came to the end of the service corridor. If their assumptions concerning the brochure map were correct, the door on the left led outside, and the door to the main shopping area was on the right near the North Pole. The only problem would be the dash through the wide open space to Macy's on the other side. One or more of the bad guys could be patrolling this end of the mall.

Apparently, Steve had been considering the same problem because he said, "What if we fly along the ceiling?"

"What?" Eric blurted. "Are you crazy? Not to mention I can't fly."

Aisha nodded. "Tim's rule number three—humans rarely look up."

"And what's the notorious accused murderer's first two rules?" Sarcasm dripped from Eric's voice.

"Always know your exits," Steve said.

"And never let anyone see you use them." Aisha grinned.

Eric glared at Steve. "If you're going to be that high, you'd better not fucking drop me."

Steve turned to Aisha. "Does he always bitch this much? He's beginning to sound like Rey."

"Hey." Aisha held up her index finger. "I said no fighting on this trip. That means Eric as well as Rey." At Eric's smirk, she jabbed her finger into his chest. "That goes for you, too. Or else, I'll tell Mom and LaShun."

"Ow." Eric rubbed the spot she'd poked. "Watch the superstrength. That hurt."

She ignored him, eased the door to the main hallway of the mall open a crack, and peeked out. The main section seemed to be deserted, and the gates and doors to all the shops locked. She waited a moment, but her HRSP-enhanced hearing only picked up noises from the end where the hostages were located. She couldn't see them because the main hallway curved as it approached the courtyard where the signing had been located. No minions poked their heads around that curve either, but they could be hiding behind the numerous kiosks filling the hallway.

Now, she kind of wished the supervillain alarm still sounded. If one of the bad guys was a super with enhanced hearing, they might hear them cross the hallway and break into Macy's.

At Steve's reminder from a moment ago, Aisha scanned the upper gallery. No lookouts stood along the railings. A little niggle of worry crawled up her spine. Either these minions were totally inept, or they had their hands full keeping the hostages under control.

"I can't see directly above us," she whispered. "There may be a lookout right overhead. Everything else seems to be clear. We might want to stay low and use the North Pole as cover."

Eric rubbed his hand over his mouth. "One of you up. One down. I'll be the distraction. If we provide multiple targets—"

"No," Aisha and Steve said at the same time.

She shook her head. "Either you stick with us, or you evacuate. I'm not explaining to my sister how I let you get killed."

"But—" Eric started.

"Aisha's right," Steve interrupted. "We do this together or not at all." He frowned at Eric. "Are you afraid of heights?"

"No." But there was a defensive tone in Eric's voice.

She exchanged a look with Steve before she returned her attention to Eric. "We need to know before we step into that hallway. If we're spotted, we're not going to have time to deal with whatever crawled up your ass."

Eric exhaled and pinched the bridge of his nose. "I'm afraid of falling, okay."

"Then boys down, girls up—" Aisha started.

"But the baby!" Eric protested.

"Chill." Steve swept Eric into his arms again. "She's invulnerable, she's fast, and she'd be the last one to unnecessarily put the baby in danger."

"Ready?" she asked.

At Steve's nod, Aisha pushed the door open. Her brothers-in-law darted around the North Pole display. She gently shut the door. The last thing they needed was any noise to attract the bad guys' attention. She launched herself straight up to the ceiling of the Upper Level.

No shouts raised the alarm. Even better, no plasma bolts targeted her while she flew across the hallway, nor did she spot anyone on the Upper Level. A metallic *crack* came from below her. She landed on the main level as Steve lifted the gate as carefully and quietly as he could manage.

Eric and Aisha slipped beneath the edge and into Macy's. Aisha held the gate so Steve could do the same. Together, they eased the gate back into place before they twisted sections of narrow slats inside the wall tracks. The damage didn't provide total security, but it would slow down any pursuers who may have seen them.

To their left was a door marked "Employees Only", so Aisha made a beeline for it, the brothers-in-law trailing behind her. It was the most logical place to start.

Of course, the door was locked. Aisha grimaced. She could hear Harri in the back of her head, bitching about the damages that taxpayers ended up covering through higher costs at retail stores because of supers. Aisha gritted her teeth and twisted the lever. The lock cracked, and she pushed the door open.

She barely got her arm up in time to block the metal pipe aimed for her head. The elf screeched as the pipe bounced off her right forearm and landed on a box.

The leg sweep Tim had taught her was awkward as hell with her over-sized abdomen, but her superstrength knocked the bastard down.

Steve grabbed the elf's collarless, striped shirt, his fist drawn back to clock the elf.

"No!" Santa Claus jumped on Steve's back, shouting "Don't you dare be naughty!"

CHAPTER 17

Harri stared at Miss Purrception, not quite believing her. "You want me to set up a meeting with your mother and daughters?"

"Well, like I said, Aisha isn't here." Miss Purrception shrugged. "My bad. I'd assumed she'd be restricted from flying at this point in her pregnancy."

Harri crossed her arms. "She also gave you the name of an attorney who specializes in the defense of supervillains."

"But he's not hosting my mother and daughters for Christmas dinner." Miss Purrception waved nonchalantly with the wine glass in her hand.

Harri held her breath as the red liquid came dangerously close to sloshing over the rim. Thank goodness, Miguel talked her into keeping the original wood floors.

Releasing the air in her lungs, she shook her head. "I can't just spring you on Rue Liberty and the girls, especially on Christmas. That could cause more harm than good to whatever relationship you want to salvage with them."

"That's only the first part of my request," Miss Purrception said. "I also want you to negotiate my surrender to the FBI the day after Christmas."

Harri dropped her arms to her side and stalked over to the kitchen cupboards. "I need my own glass of wine if we're going to talk about this." She retrieved another goblet and crossed to the island. Once she poured a rather healthy serving and took a gulp of wine, she eyed Miss Purrception.

"First of all, how did you know Rue Liberty and the girls would be here for Christmas dinner?"

"Don't worry." Muss Purrception grinned from across the island. "I didn't break your security. Your man Arthur is excellent by the way. If he wasn't so smitten with your assistant, I'd hire him away in a heartbeat."

"How is Patty stopping you?"

"Not her." Miss Purrception sipped her wine. "Her ex. I don't need Black Death crawling up my tail. Especially since we'll end up in the same prison." She waved her free hand. "Anyway, I found out because I have bugs on my mother. She doesn't take her archnemeses seriously. Just because they're geriatric, it doesn't mean they're helpless. I worry about her living alone. Even though my girls check in on her once a day, anything could happen, from a supervillain wanting revenge to falling and breaking her hip."

Harri swallowed a groan. The last thing she needed tonight was a heart-to-heart conversation with any supervillain, much less someone Tim had done the mattress mambo with. Or should that be the rooftop rumba? Aisha was in trouble, and Tim would be coming back up to the loft any minute with news of the events in Atlanta.

Harri leaned her elbows on the island. "Miss Purrception, you do realize I'm not a criminal defense attorney? I could accidentally screw up your case."

"No, you wouldn't." Miss Purrception's smile didn't have any tinge of an ulterior motive. In fact, it looked kind of wistful. "Rey told me what you did for him. If he trusts you, then I trust you."

Harri shook her head. There was no sense denying anything since Miss Purrception had rescued Rey from Corvus, then helped Aisha, Steve, and the Japanese Superhero Enforcement Bureau take down Professor Paranoia when he got his hooks into Rey's head.

"That kid can make anyone trust him."

Miss Purrception chuckled. "I think that's his real superpower. Besides your ex-husband is FBI, and you're on fairly decent terms with him. Between the two of you, there won't be any 'accidents'—" She made air quotes with her first two fingers of each hand. "—on my way to jail."

The groan and hum of the elevator gave Harri a couple of minutes warning. "Look, my boyfriend's on his way up to my loft. Since he's the firm's head of security I'd really not like to explain to him how a supervillain got into my place and why I'm sharing a glass of wine with said supervillain. Do you have a place to stay tonight?"

Miss Purrception shrugged again. "I'll just sleep in Aisha's loft. I can stay out of sight of the rest of your team."

"No, that won't work." Harri tried not to wince as the wheezing of the elevator stopped, meaning it reached the basement. "Our associate is bringing her family here. Her parent's mountain cabin was vandalized—"

"Corvus?" Miss Purrception resembled her daughter Sourpuss with her hackles up.

"It may just be plain old vandalism," Harri said. "With holidays, the sheriff doesn't have time to investigate—"

"What if I just sleep on your couch? It'll only be for the next couple of nights. Until you can make arrangements with Special Agent Lewis."

"No," Harri said firmly.

A sly smile crossed Miss Purrception's face. "Well, surely you don't want me around Miguel's boys. Nor will you risk your goddaughter's life or Arthur's rehabilitation with my presence."

The elevator groaned and wheezed again. Harri straightened and tried to swallow her panic. Her insecurity regarding her relationship with Tim outstripped her concern for her clients.

"You need to leave. Now."

"Oh, c'mon, Harri." Miss Purrception should have had a canary feather dangling from her lips with the coy expression on her face. "Just tell your boyfriend I'm an old friend from law school and my flight was cancelled."

Harri cocked her head as the picture snapped into place. "You knew his secret identity all along, didn't you?"

"Who's secret identity?" Miss Purrception batted her eyes, but she didn't achieve the innocent air she attempted.

"And you're the reason he freaked at the hotel," Harri accused as the elevator reached the fifth floor and stopped.

The supervillain didn't say a damn word. She merely smiled at the approaching footsteps.

"So this was never about your kids," Harri snapped.

Miss Purrception sighed. "Actually, it was about both."

The loft door rolled open.

"Harri, what have I said about setting the security system when you get—" Tim's dark blue eyes widened, and he reached into his pocket.

Harri rounded the island and held up her hands. "Before you go off half-cocked, let me—"

That was all she could get out before the Taser barbs pierced her skin and 1200 volts ripped through her body.

CHAPTER 18

The scene would have made Aisha laugh if Rey and the kids weren't a supervillain's hostages.

"Steve! No!" Aisha grabbed her brother-in-law's left arm. "Let the elf go."

He released the elf who tried to bean her. Once the elf was free and standing, Santa jumped off Steve's back.

Aisha took in the scene. Two women were also dressed as elves. Both were armed with metal pipes. No, not pipes. They'd unscrewed pieces of a couple of mobile clothing racks for their makeshift weapons. A man in a mall security uniform semi-reclined on a pile of clothing against the back wall. The left shoulder of his uniform had been scorched, and an ugly burn showed just under his left collarbone. Otherwise the room was filled with cardboard boxes and a bin of hangers.

She stared at the tall elf hugging his arms to his chest. The shock from the rack rod hitting her forearm must have hurt like hell. "Really? Do I look like a supervillain minion?"

"Sorry, darlin'," Santa said. It was a little weird hearing a Southern drawl from the holiday icon. "We ducked in here when the commotion started at the other end of the mall. Someone hit the supervillain alarm, and the doors in the department store automatically locked before we could get to the evacuation exit."

"Garth said we should hunker down in here and wait for the authorities," the blond female elf said as she waved at the guard. "If it's a robbery, the bad guys probably won't come into a supply room."

"How'd y'all get into the store?" Santa's blue eyes glinted with suspicion.

The last thing Aisha wanted was to spill her secrets, but they couldn't afford the mall employees panicking either. She raised her right hand and waggled her fingers. "HRSP. My husband and my sister's kids are some of the hostages taken at Mister Spectacular's signing."

"Your man's a super?" The brunette female elf's eyes widened.

Aisha ignored the woman. "Right now, the important thing is to get all of you out of here, and especially get some medical attention for Garth." She looked at Eric.

He rolled his eyes. "Any excuse to get rid of me, huh?"

"The guard and one elf are injured." Aisha shrugged. "Santa and the other elves are going to need help to get the injured out of here."

"Fine," Eric growled. "But if you don't get my kids back, I'll—"

"What?" Aisha snapped.

He scowled at her for a moment before he said, "I'll tell your mother."

A giggle burst from her. She couldn't help it. The picture in her head of Mom lecturing her about Jada and Devon being taken hostage was so ridiculous. But on the other hand, it's exactly what LaShun would threaten her with when they were kids. "Deal."

Aisha turned to Santa and the elves. "We need to ask one favor before we get all of you out of here."

CHAPTER 19

Harri wanted to smack Tim, but she was still lying on her loft floor, her muscles twitching.

"Stay still," he muttered as he knelt beside her and tried to remove the prongs.

"How am I supposed to stay still?" She glared up at him. "You fucking Tased me, Canyon!"

Miss Purrception rushed over. With the glimpse up the other woman's skirt, Harri was glad the supervillain was wearing panties. Miss Purrception knelt and applied one of the gel packs Harri kept on hand in her freezer to her chest.

"This will help ease the burning," the supervillain said. She had another gel pack in her left hand. "Just lie still for a moment to catch your breath."

"I've got breath," Harri snarled. "What I don't have is muscle control!"

Miss Purrception grinned. "It could be worse. You could have lost bladder control." She lifted Harri's head and placed the gel pack on the spot where her skull had hit the hardwood floor. The spot that would probably have a decent-sized lump in the morning.

"What is a supervillain doing in your loft?" Tim said through gritted teeth.

"Oh, that's hilarious, especially coming from Canyon Pointe's number-one vigilante," Miss Purrception shot back.

Tim stared at her. "I don't know what you're blabbering about."

"Collar and cuffs, sweetheart." She sneered.

Harri couldn't help it. The giggle burst out of her mouth and turned into a full-fledged guffaw at Tim's shocked expression. When her laughter finally died, she said, "Forgot to manscape down there, didn't you?"

She turned to Miss Purrception. "And really? You couldn't convince him to use a freakin' bed?"

The supervillain's mouth hung open as her attention switched to Tim, then back to Harri. "He told you that?"

"It's the twenty-first century, sweetheart." Harri grinned. "You should always know your partner's sexual history."

Tim made a low sound in his chest, not quite a growl, but close. "You feeling well enough to sit up?"

"Yeah," she said. With Tim and Miss Purrception's help, Harri made it upright though her knees still felt a little wobbly. However, she managed to hold both gel packs in place. "Get me to the couch, and then I want my wine before we sit down and discuss this situation like calm, rational adults."

"A calm, rational adult wouldn't Tase his girlfriend," Miss Purrception commented as they guided Harri to the living area.

"A calm, rational adult wouldn't break into her ex's living space and threaten his current girlfriend," Tim bit out.

"Is that what you're sore about, or is it the fact I outsmarted you?" Miss Purrception snapped.

"Don't you mean conned?" Tim looked angry enough to chew nails. God only knew what he was doing to his tooth enamel the way his jaw muscles twitched.

However, they were both giving Harri a stress headache on top of the lump on the back of her head.

"Stop it! Both of you!" She glared at the pair as she dropped on her little couch. "Where's my wine?"

While Miss Purrception trotted back to the kitchen, Tim sat next to Harri and whispered, "We need to call in reinforcements."

"I can hear you, Red!" the supervillain called from the kitchen.

"No, we don't because technically, Miss Purrception and I were discussing the firm representing her before you Tased me," Harri said dryly.

"Are you serious?" Tim's eyes widened. "She's—"

"Stop. Now." Harri started to roll her eyes, but the motion only sent an additional ache through her skull. "You have history with her. I get it. However, there's not only your opinion to take into account. There's Aisha, Rey, Steve, and the rest of the Reinhold clan I have to consider."

Tim's jaw twitched a few times before he said, "I think you're making a mistake."

"Noted, but you don't have a say in my clients. Only my partners and associates do." Harri lowered the gel pack from her chest. Scorch marks and holes marred the lovely pink silk and white cotton just above her right breast. "Shit. I can replace the shirt, but did you have to ruin the tie Jeremy handmade for me?"

"Next time don't jump between me and the target," he said through gritted teeth.

Miss Purrception circled the couch and held out a wine glass to Harri, the other one firmly in her hand. Both were refilled. "Why didn't Aisha or Rey tell me privately Canyon was still alive? They knew about my past, and they knew I was upset about the news of the Ghost Owl I's death." She plopped on Tim's recliner.

Harri looked at Tim.

"I didn't tell them, Harri," he protested. "You're the only one I've told about . . ." He glared at Miss Purrception again.

"Our past, you mean?" Miss Purrception took a drink before she continued. "I told Rey about my relationship with the Ghost Owl when I found the kid on the Indonesian offshore oil rig." She shrugged. "I figured he'd told Aisha or she figured it out on her own."

"Aisha wouldn't have said a word because Tim's also a client of ours." Harri sipped her wine before she set the glass on the end table. "Under the heading of Rey's too-good-to-be-true status, he's loyal to a fault." She smiled. "That's why he insisted on escorting you from Japan back to Singapore last fall. He'd never reveal anyone's secrets unless someone's life was on the line."

"I guess that's understandable." Miss Purrception sighed and eyed

Tim. "He did say you've been mentoring Kerry and Molly. Thank you for that."

If anything, Tim appeared even more suspicious. "You're welcome. I think."

"Well, Harri, now that he knows I'm here, can I crash on your couch?" The sly smile was back on Miss Purrception's beautiful face.

"She can't stay here!" Tim looked aghast.

"Better here where we can keep an eye on her than downstairs with Arthur," Harri said dryly. "Or are you planning to lock her up in the Owl's Nest?"

Tim scowled at them both. "Don't tempt me."

"Watching you two, I don't see how you ever thought Kerry and Molly were your daughters," Harri said.

As she planned, Miss Purrception choked on her mouthful of wine. Somehow, she kept from spraying it all over Harri's tan living room rug. She coughed a few times before she could manage to speak. "What on earth made you think you fathered my girls?"

The blush started at his neck and rapidly swept up his face until his ears were a brighter red than his hair. "I wasn't sure . . ."

"All right, you can use our couch for the next couple of nights." Harri laid the second gel pack in her lap and gently probed the back of her head. The spot was tender, but no lump so far or any blood. "However, I'm warning your mom and kids you're here. And if they agree to meeting with you, we'll do this here tomorrow evening because you are not ruining my goddaughter's first Christmas."

Miss Purrception opened her mouth, but Harri gestured sharply to cut her off.

"I'm not finished." She jabbed her right index finger in the direction of the supervillain. "As for representing you, I need to discuss this with Aisha and Susan. If either my partner or my associate has an objection, then you need to find someone else to represent you."

"Understood, and I agree to your terms." Miss Purrception nodded.

The intercom buzzed. Harri stood and tossed the gel packs on the couch before she wearily crossed to the wall unit. "Yeah."

"The Kennedys just pulled into the garage, Harri," Arthur reported. From the baby cooing in the background, he was in his apartment watching the security feeds from his own computer. "I'm on my way down."

"I'll meet you in the garage." Harri jabbed the button. Susan's family and Arthur would be easier to deal with than the mess in her own loft.

She turned back to Tim and Miss Purrception. "When Susan and I come back, we discuss the details of this little situation. Behave yourselves while I'm gone, or so help me, I'll Tase you both."

Harri headed out of her loft and for the elevator. Her body hurt too much to take the stairs.

However, by leaving Tim and Miss Purrception alone, Harri just hoped she had a loft to come back to once the Kennedys were settled.

Chapter 20

Rey held the children close as they snuggled against him. With all these hostages, he understood why Mister Spectacular didn't try to overpower the supervillain and his minions. Hell, he didn't dare make a move either. It would be too easy for someone to get hurt or killed. Part of him was happy Aisha wasn't here, but he didn't think he could face her or LaShun and Eric if something happened to Devon and Jada.

Some of the supervillain's minions had jammed the gates of the handful of stores around the courtyard or blown holes in the doors when they rushed into the mall while the others took control of the families waiting to meet Mister Spectacular. The minions then proceeded to pull out the employees and shoppers before they could escape via the evacuation routes. The odd thing was the minions weren't grabbing the cash or looting any of the stores.

"We need to do something," the dad next to him whispered, the one who had been teasing him about Aisha's pregnancy cravings.

"We have no idea what the power sets for the supervillain or his minions are." Rey whispered back. "Not to mention our children will be in the line of fire."

"All we need to do is grab one of their weapons and hold one of these assholes hostage," the other dad said.

Before Rey could reply, Devon snorted in derision. "Dude, the supervillains never care about their minions, and the other guys will cut you down before you figure out how their stupid guns work," the kid hissed.

"Son, why don't you let the grown-ups handle this?"

Even Rey bristled at the dad's patronizing tone. The unknown supervillian noticed their conversation and strode in their direction.

"What's the problem over here?" The supervillain's tone was even more patronizing than the other dad's.

"I have to pee," Jada wailed.

The other kids around them took up the cry.

"I have to go, too!"

"Me, too!"

"I really have to poop."

It would have been funny if the stakes weren't everyone's lives.

"None of you are leaving this area!" The supervillain shouted, which prompted some of the younger children to start crying.

"Look." Rey held up his hands to show he had no weapons. "Let one of the parents and one of your . . . employees take the kids in small batches to use the employee restroom in one of the closer stores. Otherwise, it's going to get very smelly in this courtyard before you're finished with whatever you have planned."

"And I suppose, you want to take the kids?" The supervillain sneered under his garish orange mask. *Dios*, it was almost as bad as the yellow and green spandex Rey used when he first made himself public as a super.

"Most people on the street avoid me because of my size." He shrugged. "I don't expect you to trust me. There's lots of other parents here to choose from."

"No, I think we'll make this easier on me." The supervillain pointed his index finger at Devon and gestured for him to approach. "Come here. You'll stay with me while your daddy takes everyone else to the potty."

Devon looked up at Rey, fright written all over the boy's face.

"It's okay, Devon." Rey turned and glared at the unknown supervillain. "He won't hurt you. If he does, he won't have any leverage against the other parents here."

Something flickered in the supervillain's eyes. Why was he more worried about the parents than the cops or the superheroes? That didn't make any sense.

Rey carefully disengaged himself from the kids and stood with his hands raised. "How many at a time?"

"Six."

"All right." Rey reached down and helped Jada to her feet. Her chin jutted forward, but she wisely said nothing as she stared at the supervillain.

"She's one," Rey said loudly. "Count off toward the front of the line."

"No!" The supervillain jabbed his index finger toward the people behind Rey and the kids in line.

"Look, I get that you don't have children." Once again, Rey caught something in the supervillain's gaze. This time, it seemed to be pain. "The kids closer to the head of the line have been at the mall and standing here longer. They have smaller bladders than the adults. Unless you want messes, those kids need to go first."

"Well, aren't you just parent of the year?" The supervillain scowled and leaned closer to Rey. "You contradict me again, and I'll burn your son's face off."

"Understood," Rey bit out. He continued to meet the masked villain's gaze while he said, "Kids, count off."

"One," Jada called out. The next five kids followed her lead.

"All of you stick close to me. And don't make any sudden moves. We don't want any misunderstandings." Rey took Jada's hand and headed for the shoe store. The other five kids and one of the armed minions followed them.

"Uncle Rey," Jada whispered as they walked past displays of the latest designer sneakers. "Something's not right here."

"No, it's not," he said, trying to be as soothing as possible. It's what Aisha would have done if she were here. "But I'll make sure you're safe."

"No, I mean the bad guy didn't declare who he was." She glanced over her shoulder at the minion following them. "Mister Spectacular doesn't know who he is either. And aren't the supervillains supposed to be all about riches, revenge, and world domination?"

Damn, Jada was smart. A niggle of worry ran through Rey. How would he keep up with his own son if a twelve-year-old girl was bright enough to realize this wasn't the usual hostage bullshit Tim had taught him about?

"Most of the time," he whispered back.

They reached the store room. Luckily, the employees didn't have a chance to lock it. The last thing he could do was display his powers.

"What are you two whispering about?" the minion behind them snapped.

Rey paused and looked at the minion while the kids headed toward the employee bathroom. "My daughter started her first period." He tilted his head. "She's a little freaked. Do you have to be an asshole about this?"

An uncomfortable expression crossed the minion's face. "You deal with it. I'll wait out here, but don't you dare close this door. I've been itching to test this baby on a live target." He pivoted sharply and stalked out of the stock room.

"What do we do, Uncle Rey?" Jada whispered.

"I don't know yet." He looked around the storeroom. A landline telephone sat on a desk amid a lot of paperwork and a couple of boxes of shoes. Who would he call? Aisha and Steve were the only supers he knew in Atlanta, and he prayed his brother was keeping his wife safe.

Damn, Tim would know how to improvise with the material in here, but short of throwing shoes at the minions . . .

Wait a minute. That could actually work.

If he could get the child hostages away from the minions first.

Rey grinned at his niece. "Jada, when we go back out there, spread the word that I need shoes."

She cocked her head. "What's wrong with yours?"

"I need things to throw at the bad guys," he said.

"I can help," another girl piped up. "I can throw a mean fast ball. Close to eighty miles per hour."

"Not as fast as this guy can, I'll bet." An older boy gestured at Rey. "Haven't you noticed he's the only parent who isn't afraid of the bad guys? You're special, aren't you?"

"Keep your voices down," Rey murmured. He needed some allies, and maybe, just maybe, his *loco* plan might work and not get anybody killed.

The older boy's little brother tugged on the right leg of Rey's jeans. "Tell us what else you need, sir."

"And we promise we won't out your secret identity," the girl with the wicked fast ball said.

"For right now, I just need as many shoes as I can get without anyone getting the bad guy's attention." Rey grinned at the kids. "The bigger the better."

"Any shoes with sharp pointy heels would work, too," the third girl said. She poked at her glasses.

"Yep, those would definitely work," Rey said. "Everybody needs to use the restroom. We don't want to rouse suspicion."

In five minutes, the kids marched out of the storeroom behind Rey. He took two more sets of children into the shoe storm employee bathroom. As they came out, there was a ruckus coming from the minions guarding the hallway that led to the main section of the mall.

Rey's heart tried to climb out of his throat. Despite the half-assed mask that didn't match any of the other minions' disguises, he would have recognized the build, height, and gait of his twin brother anywhere. But it was the bound figure in the Santa suit, wig, and beard that sent his heart into overdrive.

Aisha.

Chapter 21

Aisha tried to smooth down the artificial white curls that kept trying to climb up her nostrils. The Santa suit was the only thing that would fit her, and she needed something to hide her face. However, wearing the damn fake beard was worse than kissing Rey with full facial hair.

That thought plucked at her heart. He'd make sure Devon and Jada were safe. She just prayed no one was hurt besides the three people she saw sprawled on the mall floor.

Steve re-entered the supply closet/dressing room.

"Any problems?" she asked.

He shook his head and stepped behind some boxes to change. "Eric was still complaining about being tricked into leaving, but Santa and the elves were relieved to be out of here. FYI, it sounds like the supervillain is delaying the negotiator."

"How do you know?" she asked.

"I heard part of the conversation when the SWAT unit swarmed Eric and the other folks." His voice was muffled for the last part of the sentence, but the rest of what he said was perfectly clear. "One of the other Atlanta superheroes is out in the parking lot, too. He's arguing with the police about rushing the villain and his minions, but he doesn't sound sober. The weird part is the bad guys left the security cameras on, but no one seems to know who this supervillain is."

That part worried Aisha as well. This was sounding less and less like a robbery or the usual supervillain challenge to authority. "Did the police see you?"

"No. And I'm not sure I want to be seen in this outfit." Steve stepped from behind the boxes wearing the male elf's attire.

She had to bite her tongue to keep from laughing. Steve's body was far more muscular than the male elf's though they were about the same height. Unfortunately, the outfit put *all* of Steve on display. Aunt Queenie would have a field day seeing Steve in the elf costume.

"Here's a mask I found in the leftover Halloween merchandise." She handed him the glittery emerald mask. Unfortunately, it was only held in place with an elastic band.

He put it on and pulled the jingly elf cap on top of his head. "You really think this is going to disguise my identity?"

"Sweetie, no one's going to be looking at your face." She pivoted and marched out of the supply closet/dressing room before her laughter could start.

"Hey! What's that supposed to mean?" He scurried after her.

"It means don't wear that outfit around Aunt Queenie, or I'm not responsible for what she does to you."

<hr>

Sticking to their plan, Steve borrowed a scarf from Macy's to tie Aisha's hands and led her down the hallway toward the courtyard where Mister Spectacular's signing had been. As they neared Bloomingdale's, another man dressed as an elf popped out from behind a kiosk. He was holding some kind of rifle-like weapon, but Aisha could hear a high-pitched electric hum coming from it.

"Where the hell have you been? And where's the mask the boss gave you?"

"Santa here ripped it off." Steve jerked Aisha forward. "I scrounged another one."

Alarm shone in the minion's eyes. "Did the security cameras catch your face?"

"No, he was hiding in one of the dressing rooms," Steve replied.

The minion frowned beneath his mask. "Why didn't he leave with the rest of the evacuees?"

Steve shrugged. "He caught me doubling back."

Aisha's stomach lurched as she put together what Steve had already deduced. The male elf with Eric was one of the supervillain's crew.

The minion in front of them shook his head. The bell on his cap jingled. "I guess one more hostage won't hurt, but I don't know how killing this one is going to play on the CCTV."

Now, her stomach tried to escape up her esophagus. Even the baby stilled inside of her. This whole situation was worse than she had believed.

"That's the boss's decision, not ours," Steve said. "We don't get paid enough for that."

"Losing your guts over this already?" The minion sneered.

"Nope." Steve shrugged again. "I just know my place in the hierarchy."

"Oooo! Look at the big man with the big words."

"You just watch for the cops and the supers," Steve snapped. "I need to deposit this one with the rest of the hostages."

The minion made a face, but he didn't add any other insults while Steve jerked Aisha in the direction of the signing.

"This isn't good," he murmured in her ear.

"This isn't a simple hostage situation," Aisha whispered. "They're here to make some kind of statement."

"Yeah, the wrong kind."

The hall turned to the left. Aisha guesstimated around two hundred worried and scared people sat on the floor. A bit of relief went through her when she spotted Jada in the same spot where she'd left her to buy the toddler t-shirt.

But where the hell was Rey?

Mister Spectacular stood next to the villain Karen had described as being the opposite of the superhero. Where Mister Spectacular's outfit was red and blue, the supervillain's was a garish green and orange. And she realized why Mister Spectacular hadn't done a damn thing. Stationed around the courtyard were eight minions dressed as mall elves with weapons pointed at the heads of the children they held.

Not eight. She spotted Devon. The unknown supervillain had a tight hold on her nephew. She hadn't spotted him right away because of the stacks of photos and comics on the table for Mister Spectacular to sign.

Aisha's blood chilled. Even with their superspeed, the odds were one of the children would die if she, Rey, and Steve tried to rush the minions at the same time, and that was assuming Rey was all right. He wouldn't have left the kids unless he was forced to. She prayed an opportunity would present itself before the supervillain executed his plan, and the civilians here all died.

Including Devon and Jada.

<h1 style="text-align:center">CHAPTER 22</h1>

Once they got Susan's parents settled in her apartment's spare bedroom and her sister's family in Aisha's place, Harri dragged an exhausted Susan over to her loft.

"How much criminal defense work have you done?" Harri asked.

"Not a whole lot." Susan rubbed her right eye with the heel of her hand. "Mainly criminal mischief or vandalism regarding the misuse of superpowers. Anyone we know get a holiday DUI?"

"More serious than that," Harri muttered as she rolled back her loft door and gestured for their associate to enter.

"Hey, Tim!" Susan said cheerfully.

Harri wasn't sure where Susan's sudden energy came from. One second she could barely put one foot in front of the other, the next she turned on the charm, suspecting a potential client was involved.

Susan crossed over to Miss Purrception, her hand extended and a bright smile on her face despite the dark circles under her eyes. "Hello, I'm Susan Kennedy, Winters & Franklin's only associate."

"Miss Purrception," the supervillain answered.

Susan didn't miss a step, but then she'd been working on her own for the last few years. "Harri didn't have a chance to fill me in yet. What can we do for you, Miss Purrception?"

"I've asked for Harri's assistance to see my family on Christmas before I turn myself into the feds."

"Don't forget needing a place to sleep," Tim muttered.

Susan looked at Harri, who shook her head.

"Never mind him," Harri said.

"Is there a reason she needs my couch instead of yours?" Susan asked.

"It's not a good idea. Mom's already wound up about the change in holiday plans."

"Nope, Miss Purrception is going to take Steve's room for the next couple of nights."

"She's sleeping on the damn couch," Tim sputtered.

Miss Purrception snickered.

"You want to make it the floor?" he growled.

Harri could practically see the lightbulb explode inside Susan's brain as she put two and two together.

Susan shrugged. "Sorry, Miss Purrception, I'm not trying to be rude, but my mother is in the beginning stages of dementia. Having Christmas here may be rough as it is."

"You know you and your family are eating with us," Harri stated firmly.

"And we appreciate the invite." A rueful smile crossed Susan's face. "But don't get offended if Dad and I end up taking our meals downstairs with Mom."

Harri put on her best pleading face. "Actually, I was hoping your parents could help keep Qiang's dad occupied during Christmas Day."

"Qiang's dad?" Susan shot the briefest of worried looks at Miss Purrception. "Why—oh, crap. Her mom had another stroke?"

"Yeah." Harri hugged herself. "Qiang can't get him to eat much, and he won't go home to get some rest. He just catnaps in the recliner in her mom's hospital room. Connor is staying with Miguel for the holidays."

Susan nodded, a thoughtful expression on her face. "That might work in both of our favors. He'll give Mom someone to fuss over instead of stewing about her own problems."

"Oh, my god," Miss Purrception blurted.

They both turned to look at the supervillain.

"It's not just Rey." She stared at Harri and Susan with a mix of wonder and contempt. "You are all a bunch of goodie-two-shoes."

"No," Tim growled. "They're a family. They look out for each other. That's something beyond your comprehension."

"Now, just a minute—" Miss Purrception started to rise from the recliner.

"Sit down," Harri barked. "Tomorrow, I need to run out and get Connor's gifts—"

"I can do that for you," Miss Purrception said.

"You cannot be seen in public until we negotiate your surrender to the FBI." Harri cocked her head. "Or are you reneging on that?"

"No," the supervillain said sullenly as she sat back down.

"Ah, that's why you were asking me about criminal defense," Susan said.

"Sorry for making you work on Christmas Eve," Harri said. "But I need you to start lining things up for Miss Purrception's surrender while I get Qiang's shopping done first thing in the morning."

"What are we going to do with her in the meantime?" Susan nodded toward the supervillain. "Technically, if she stays here, we're harboring a wanted criminal."

"She's going to work off part of her attorney fees by doing some dinner prep work—" Harri started.

"That's not what we agreed to!" Miss Purrception protested.

Harri ignored her and continued, "—while Tim watches her, and I try to set up a meeting with her family."

Miss Purrception jumped to her feet. The only reason wine didn't slosh out of her glass was because she'd drank it all. "That's involuntary servitude!"

Harri crossed her arms. "Then you have two other choices. You can leave, or I get out my Taser." She shot Miss Purrception a malicious grin. "And mine is designed to take down Rey."

Fine," the supervillain muttered and sat back down in the recliner.

"Uh, Harri, were you cooking tonight?" Susan stared at Harri's chest.

"No. Why?"

"Just wondering why you have burn marks on your tie and shirt?"

Tim groaned. Miss Purrception snickered some more.

"That's a misunderstanding," Harri said. "We've got a bigger problem."

"Bigger than a supervillain drinking wine in your living room?" Susan's right eyebrow rose.

"Yeah, Aisha and Rey are in the middle of a hostage situation at an Atlanta mall."

CHAPTER 23

"Thanks, Betty. I'll call once we know something from our end." Harri thumbed the icon to end the call and turned to the folks in her living room. "Aisha, Rey, and Steve left for Lenox Square with Eric and his kids to do some last minute shopping and for Devon to get Mister Spectacular's autograph a little before four p.m. local time. The breaking news report came on the Atlanta news stations about an hour and a half later."

Sitting beside Tim on the couch, Arthur nodded. "That matches what I've learned. The supervillain alarm went off at five-forty-six Eastern Standard Time." He had come up to the loft with his laptop shortly after Susan's arrival. "According to the mall security cameras, the attackers had control of the courtyard before anyone sounded the alarm."

"What are they doing?" Tim frowned. "Are their accomplices stealing while the others are holding the hostages?"

"There's been no other detectable movement in the other parts of the mall," Arthur answered.

"What do you mean by detectable movement?" Harri leaned over the guy's shoulders to see the screen.

Arthur tapped some keys, and the scene switched. "This is the recording outside of Macy's two hours ago."

A large kiosk sat in the middle of the mall's hallway. Above a throne, a sign that said, "North Pole," topped a huge backdrop. What looked to be velvet ropes hooked to metal stands enclosed the area. More of the crowd control devises marked the places for customers to line up. Some of the stands and the camera to take pictures of kids on Santa's lap had been knocked over, probably when shoppers and clerks panicked at hearing people screaming and the supervillain alarm.

"I'm not seeing anything, Arthur," Harri said.

"Maybe you need to get your reading glasses," Miss Purrception suggested as she refilled her wine glass at the kitchen island.

Harri bit her tongue from answering in kind. It figured the supervillain had searched her loft. Harri reminded herself that she was the younger woman in this pathetic love triangle.

"Let me rewind and slow this down frame-by-frame," Arthur muttered. On the first frame, a door between two stores on the left side of the screen seemed to open by itself.

Arthur clicked a button for the next still picture. This time the door was closed. "Here." His index finger traced two faint blurry lines. "These appear to be two separate entities moving at superspeed as they exit from the service corridor."

"Wait a minute." Miss Purrception joined them to stand beside Harri and leaned over Arthur's right shoulder. "Look how the blur to the North Pole display is almost as wide as it is tall. That person is carrying someone or something."

Susan joined them to watch Arthur's screen over the back of the couch. "Did someone get hurt?"

"I don't think so." Arthur tapped the key for the next frame. The image clearly showed one of the twins kneeling and fiddling with the lock on the Macy's security gate. Eric Simmons, Aisha's brother-in-law, peered around the edge of the department store's faux-marble façade, looking in the direction where the hostages were being kept.

"LaShun's husband isn't a super," Harri added. "That's why he was being carried."

The third frame showed the gate back in place. The face behind it didn't have a beard.

"That's Steve," Tim said.

"What's he doing to the gate?" Susan asked.

"Since he probably broke the lock to get Eric inside, he's jamming the gate to slow down the perps," Tim muttered.

"That doesn't explain where Rey, Aisha, and the kids are," Harri said.

"Unfortunately, we know where three of them are located." Arthur tapped some more keys. "This is one of the feeds from the courtyard where the hostages are being held."

Harri's blood turned to ice when she recognized Rey, Jada, and Devon. The kids were trying to put on brave faces in front of their superhero uncle. Rey, on the other hand, looked downright pissed.

"I'm guessing the second blur in the Macy's section was Aisha," Arthur said.

"Thank goodness, we can keep an eye on them, even if we can't do much," Susan murmured. "Do we have any contacts among the Atlanta supers?"

"No." Harri shook her head as she continued to stare at the screen. "Ultramegaperson is making some calls on our behalf, but they haven't called me back yet."

"That's what doesn't make sense," Arthur said as he waved at the screen. "If it were me, the first thing I'd do is cut the video feeds."

"I've got to concur with Mr. Drallhickey," Miss Purrception said. "Last thing I'd want is the cops knowing all my movements."

Tim looked up at Harri, the same suspicion in his eyes.

"Fuck!" She slapped her hands against the back couch cushions. "This isn't the usual robbery or extortion bullshit. They're planning to kill the hostages, and they want everyone to see it."

Chapter 24

Aisha kept her head down and observed everything through her lashes as Steve dragged her toward the direction of Jada. Thank goodness, she'd given up wearing much makeup during the latest three months of her pregnancy. The damn hormones had her sweating like crazy.

Like they did, right now.

"Well, what do we have here?" The unknown supervillain sauntered up to Steve and Aisha, dragging Devon along.

Her nephew eyed her suspiciously until she winked. The fear in his expression didn't totally fade, but there was a hint of relief in his eyes.

"Santa here decided to play hero," Steve grumbled. "Sit down there." He jerked her toward Jada.

Like her brother, Aisha's niece looked at her with a bit of suspicion until Aisha winked at her, too. Jada's eyes widened, but she managed to stay still and silent.

"Did you get the charges set?" the supervillain snapped.

"No. I had my hands a little full." Irritation oozed from Steve.

The supervillain's eyes narrowed behind his mask. "You look bigger than you did in street clothes."

Panic plucked at Aisha's nerves. Did she grab Devon and Jada and try to fly them out of here? That action would leave everyone else's children behind. Guilt wouldn't let her do that. Not to another mother.

"What the fuck, man?" Steve cocked his head. "Are you actually trying to pick me up here and now?"

"What? No!" The unknown supervillain took a step away from Steve. "And watch your language. There are little kids here. Jamison!"

Another minion trotted over to them. "Go help Randy here finish setting the charges."

Minion Jamison set off down the main hallway. After a split-second's hesitation, Steve followed him. He could make sure the minion never set these charges. If they could pick off one minion at a time, maybe they'd have a chance to get the hostages out of here alive.

Crap! Where was Rey?

A group of kids exited the shoe store across the courtyard shepherded by her husband and another minion.

Rey studiously ignored Aisha as the children returned to their parents. "Next group, sound off."

"No!" The supervillain dragged Devon in Rey's direction. "The rest of them can stay right here."

"Fine." Rey shrugged. "Then you don't need my son."

"You want him back so bad? I think I'll keep him for right now. Go sit down with your daughter and Santa." Once Rey complied, the unknown supervillain hauled Devon around the circle of hostages and back to where he was standing next to Mister Spectacular.

"I hope you have a plan, Santa," Rey whispered.

"I did until I knew explosives were involved," Aisha whispered back.

"We need more help than Hunahpu."

Aisha smiled underneath her fake beard at Rey's use of his brother's Mayan name, but she understood why. The parents and children around them were paying a little too close attention to their conversation.

"We've got some shoes," Jada whispered. She lifted the edge of Rey's discarded jacket. There was a small pile of shoes.

"Shoes?" Aisha mouthed.

He shrugged. "I was working with what I had. Steve should have gotten you and Eric out of here."

"I'm assuming you don't have your phone," Aisha whispered.

Rey gave a slight shake of his head.

"They confiscated everyone's when they grabbed us," the father on her left side murmured, the one who had been teasing Rey when she left them to buy the toddler t-shirt. "But they didn't take our wallets, which doesn't make sense if this is a robbery gone wrong."

"The bird call app?" Rey's right eyebrow rose.

Arthur, bless him, had created an app based on Tim's sonic emitter. Their phones didn't have the range of the actual weapon, but it could buy time in an emergency.

"That's what I was planning, but Hunahpu still has his on him." She gave a slight shake of her head. "We need more than just mine."

The skin on the back out her neck prickled despite the heat of the stupid wig. Both the unknown supervillain and a couple of the minions were looking at them.

"Silence your phone." Rey barely breathed the words.

"Already did," she said.

"Text I.T. See if he can access the security cameras. If so, have him set off all three of our phones when Hunahpu comes back."

"We're still outnumbered."

"No, you're not," the father sitting next to her whispered. Several of the parents around them nodded once, even if they weren't looking directly at Aisha.

"Give me the phone," Jada whispered. "They're keeping too close an eye on you."

Which was true. And Aisha sure as hell couldn't text while tied up and with the Santa gloves on her hands. Not without drawing more attention than she already was.

She slipped her phone from inside the borrowed left boot and slid it under her right thigh. Jada shifted and used her foot to scoot the phone under her body.

Someone grabbed the back of the fuzzy white collar and dragged Aisha backward. With the red fake fur pants, she slid across the linoleum tiles.

One of the minions pointed his weapon at her face. "What do you think you're doing?"

She lowered her voice an octave. "Just reassuring the children. You're scaring them."

"Do you see any supers around?" the minion mocked.

"Mister Spectacular's here."

"And has he done jackshit?" The minion pressed a button on the side of his weapon, and it hummed to life. "How do you think these rugrats would react if I shoot Santa Claus in the face?"

CHAPTER 25

Harri wanted to hit something. Anything. But she didn't have time to run down to the gym and wear herself out on Tim's punching bags. She needed to keep it together in front of staff and clients.

"So what do we do?" Susan asked. "It would take Blue Racer eight hours at top speed to run from Canyon Pointe to Atlanta. By then, the situation would be resolved one way or the other."

"Let me think—" The music on her cell phone saved Harri from coming up with an instant solution out of her ass. Blood roared in her head when she saw who the call was from. She swiped the green icon to answer.

"Eric, what the hell—"

"Shut up, Harri," he snapped. "I don't have much time."

"Let me put you on speaker. Everybody's in my loft because we saw or heard the news." She tapped another icon. "Okay, go."

"I already called LaShun. Rey and the kids are with the rest of the hostages. The other two think they can pull off a rescue."

The authorities must be standing nearby for Eric not to use Aisha and Steve's names.

"The only official super in there is Mister Spectacular. I got a handful of people out, including an injured security guard." Eric's voice broke. "Harri, how do we save my kids?"

"Which supers have arrived on the scene?" she asked.

"Only General Lee so far because of the holidays." Eric lowered his voice. "And I swear to God, Harri, he's useless. Even I can smell he's been celebrating a little too early. One of the lady officers is keeping him out of everyone's way."

"Can you ask the police to sit tight?" she said. "Ultramegaperson is calling in some favors from our end."

"I didn't know you knew them." Eric sounded confused.

"Friend of a friend situation," Harri replied.

"I hate standing here and not being able to do anything," Eric growled.

"Welcome to the club." Harri laughed. "Get the police to delay if you can. Is it okay if I give Ultramegaperson your number? It'll be easier than going through me."

"Sure." Eric hesitated before he added, "Thanks, Harri."

As soon as she ended the call, her ring tone warbled again. "Speak of the devil," she muttered before she swiped to answer the next call. "What have you got for me, Ultra?"

"Glass is on her way back to Atlanta, but she's still an hour out when I spoke with her," Ultramegaperson said breathlessly. "She already spoke with the SWAT team leader on sight. The cops are keeping a lid on General Lee. The old bastard is drunk again. The NSB should have forcibly retired him years ago." They paused. "I'm sorry, Harri. It's the best we can do at the moment."

"Glass needs to know the truth, Harri," Miss Purrception said.

"Missy?" Ultramegaperson sounded shocked.

"Long story," Miss Purrception said. "Harri's not doing anything wrong, and you'll see it in the papers the day after Christmas." She sucked in a deep breath as if she expected Harri to end the call and do something to her.

"Glass will have some help," Miss Purrception said in a rush. "The new Ghost Owl is inside Lenox Square Mall with their family."

"The *new* Ghost Owl? The one who took out the fake Captain Justice?" Disbelief tinged Ultramegaperson's voice.

"We're in the process of registering Ghost Owl," Harri said. The last thing she wanted was a prospective client thinking her firm promoted vigilantism.

"How will Glass be able to identify Ghost Owl if they're in civilian clothing?" Ultramegaperson asked.

"Because Ghost Owl is now sitting with the hostages dressed as Santa Claus," Arthur blurted.

CHAPTER 26

Steve followed Jamison down to the Plaza Level. The minion headed straight for California Pizza Kitchen, which stood directly below the interior courtyard holding all the hostages. A sick feeling ran through Steve.

Like he was trapped in a perverse reality version of "Die Hard." So, how were the bad guys planning to escape? The authorities had to have surrounded the mall by now.

For the love of all that was holy, he was only twenty-one. He was supposed to be starting law school next month, not trying to outwit a bunch of psycho terrorists. Because that's all these assholes were. And he'd already been fooled by the douchebag he let out of the mall with Eric.

But if this situation had happened at his parents during Thanksgiving in Seattle, Rey and Aisha would be doing their damnedest to save his little cousins. Right now, his brother and sister-in-law depended on him since he was the only one free, and he would not, could not, let them down.

Inside the restaurant, Jamison said, "I'll get the ones on the right. You get the ones on the left."

Shit. Steve looked around the dining area. Where the hell were the explosives supposed to be?

"Why the hell are you screwing around?" Jamison stood on a chair. He was doing something behind one of the fake hanging plants. "Boss can only stall that negotiator for a little bit longer before they send in another super."

"But there's plenty of us to handle anyone who tries to be a hero, including the douche in spandex upstairs," Steve said as he dragged a chair over to the closest fake pothos on the left side of the dining area.

"That ain't the plan, man, and you know it," Jamison said.

Steve climbed up on the chair. As much as the idea of what his brother and friends did made him uncomfortable, he was glad Tim had showed him some basics about explosives. A black rectangular box was attached to the wall. At first glance, it would look like a portable wireless speaker. He lifted the box from its hanger and popped the cover off the back.

Alarm ran through him at the sight of the slightly off-white putty inside the black plastic. C4. His political science and business degrees didn't prepare him for this kind of trouble.

However, Tim said the good thing about plastic explosives were their stability. A simple switch inside the casing only needed to be flipped to arm the detonator. Wires poked into the putty from the switch.

Steve glanced over at Jamison, but the minion had moved to the next plant. Sucking in a deep breath, Steve broke the switch and yanked the wires out of the putty. After carefully cracking the circuit board to disable it, he tucked the wires and circuit board into the hanging planter.

He took his time going to the next set of fake greenery. No sense arousing the minion's suspicions by moving too fast. He repeated disabling each device and hiding the wires and broken circuit boards under the fake moss inside the planters.

When he met Jamison at the last fake pothos, he had the next step of his plan. "You know some of the guys upstairs are getting squirrely about killing the hostages."

"You one of them?"

"No, but the boss wants all the loose ends tied up," Steve said.

"You're right, kid." Jamison pointed his weapon at Steve. "Too bad you're a loose end."

A blinding blast of light and heat hit Steve in the chest.

CHAPTER 27

Harri stared at Arthur. "You can't be serious?"

"I'm watching the Ghost Owl on the security camera feed." He turned his laptop so she could see the screen. In addition to the feed from the courtyard, he now had another window open showing Steve and another minion walking toward the escalator inside the mall.

But sure enough, someone in a Santa suit sat next to Jada and Rey. It looked like Santa was the only one of the hostages who'd been restrained, their hands tied by what appeared to be a scarf. Where was Devon though? As Harri watched, one of the minions stalked over and grabbed Santa by the back of her coat.

Aisha and the minion appeared to exchange words before the minion aimed his weapon at her face.

"Oh, shit," Harri muttered. She couldn't look away from the screen. Oh, please, let her be invulnerable to whatever that weapon did. But if the weapon didn't affect her, the gig was up.

The minion turned away from Aisha and talked to someone off screen. Slowly, he lowered his weapon, but his action didn't stop the pounding of Harri's blood in her ears.

"Just a second, Harri," Ultramegaperson said. "Glass is calling me." The signal clicked. After a couple of seconds, the superhero was back on the line. "Anything else we need to relay to her? She can't take her phone with her into the mall."

Despite her fear, Harri noticed Ultramegaperson was being misleading about Glass's actual location. From a safety issue, Harri understand why the supers didn't want anyone to know their exact position, but Glass had to be closer than the hour Ultramegaperson had indicated earlier. The lack of specific knowledge was frustrating as hell, but if Glass could help Aisha and the guys, Harri needed to keep her worry to herself and give what information she had.

"Only that Owl has a super friend who is now disguised as one of the elves like the rest of the minions, so Glass has backup. We lost sight of him when he entered the California Pizza Kitchen on the Plaza Level with another one of the minions. Also, she can question Eric Simmons." Harri rattled off Eric's phone number. "He's a civilian on site who got the real Santa, an injured security guard, and three elves out of the mall."

"The real Santa?" Disbelief ran through Ultramegaperson's voice.

"The guy the mall hired for the North Pole photo opportunities," Harri snapped.

"Chill, Harri." Ultramegaperson laughed. "At the rate you've been exposing urban myths, I had to ask." Thankfully, they knew better than to ask how Harri knew Eric.

Harri blew out a deep breath. "Sorry, I know two of the kids who are hostages."

"Understood," Ultramegaperson murmured. "You know Glass and Ghost Owl will do their best to get everyone out safely."

"I know." A lump rose in Harri's throat, and she swallowed hard to get it out of the way. "Thank you for everything."

"I'll call you when I know something." At Ultramegaperson's words, the line went dead.

"You didn't tell them CJ was on site," Miss Purrception said.

"Captain Justice is dead, remember?" Harri tried to figure out what the supervillain's game was. "Besides, you didn't say anything either."

Miss Purrception raised her glass. "Hey, I like the kid. I'm not outing him. Did he re-register?"

Harri smiled despite herself. "You know I can't discuss other clients with you."

"As an accused supervillain, I can appreciate attorney-client privilege." Miss Purrception grinned.

"We've got eyes on Devon, Harri," Tim said.

Everyone crowded around Arthur and his laptop. The guy in the outfit matching Mister Spectacular's had what appeared to be a firm grip on Devon's elbow.

The minion who threatened to shoot Aisha jerked her to her feet. They walked along with the supervillain and Devon off camera.

Harri had been worried about surviving Christmas. Now, she wondered if some of the people she loved would make it to Christmas Eve Day.

Chapter 28

Aisha didn't fight the minion as he guided her over to the table where the villains made Mister Spectacular sit. As much as she wanted to deck the asshole who threated to shoot her in the face, she couldn't put Devon in danger.

Mister Spectacular examined her with cool blue eyes while they approached, but he said nothing. He'd probably been told the minions would kill one of the hostages if he so much as opened his mouth.

He was one of the few superheroes who didn't wear a mask. His parents and siblings had died in the chemical explosion that bestowed his powers on him. His only other relative, his maternal grandmother, had passed away shortly after he turned eighteen. He decided to live his superhero life full-time.

Aisha didn't think she could do that. She needed some semblance of a private life, a lesson she'd learned through both her father and her ex-husband's public service. But her wishes meant nothing if she didn't get her family out of this situation.

She allowed the minion to slam her into the chair next to Mister Spectacular.

An instant later, another mother who'd been sitting relatively close to Rey and the kids stood. "Hey, what about taking the rest of our kids to the bathroom?"

"Shut the fuck up, and sit down." The minion who'd threatened Aisha stalked toward the woman. The unknown supervillain dragged Devon in that direction. Whatever happened before she arrived in the Santa suit, the villain didn't trust Rey. Not that she wanted her husband hurt, but he was more likely to survive one of those plasma bolts than her nephew was.

"You aren't Dennis," Mister Spectacular whispered.

"Who?" Aisha whispered back.

"Lenox Square's regular Santa."

Her lips quirked beneath her borrowed beard. "No."

"Super?"

"Yes."

In the middle of the hostages, the mother attempted to negotiate more bathroom breaks.

Mister Spectacular shot a quick glance at Aisha before scowling at the unknown supervillain again. "Anyone I know?"

"Not personally." For an instant, she hesitated before she said, "Don't flip out on me. Ghost Owl."

"One or two?"

"Two. In the process of registering."

Despite the scowl, one corner of Mister Spectacular's mouth quirked. "After the baby you mean?"

Aisha froze. Somehow, she kept from looking at the superhero. "How'd you know?"

"You feel like two people to me instead of one." So, Mister Spectacular's vaunted extra-sensory perception was everything it was reported to be.

"Arthur lost Steve on the camera when they entered the California Pizza Kitchen," Jada murmured.

Aisha nodded once to let her niece and Rey know she heard the news.

"What's your move, Owl?" Mister Spectacular whispered.

"Waiting for a third super to come back, so there's four of us."

The superhero's eyes widened slightly. "One of the minions downstairs?"

Again, she gave a slight nod.

"What's the signal?"

"Sonic device on my phone." She smiled underneath the fake beard. "You won't miss it."

Rey held Jada close against him to hide her texting, but the minion with the attitude must have seen something because he rushed in their direction.

"Stop texting," Aisha whispered, but it was too late for Rey to relay the message or hide the phone.

The minion reached down and grabbed Aisha's phone from Jada and pointed his weapon at the girl.

CHAPTER 29

Steve stumbled backward and flailed before he crashed into the table and chairs behind him. The ugly smell of burning synthetic material stung his nostrils.

Jamison stepped forward, his weapon raised, and blinked in surprise. "You're a super?"

Steve patted the smoldering bits of material left on his torso. His skin was pink, and his chest hair was singed. Otherwise, the idiotic elf costume had taken the brunt of the plasma bolt.

He grinned up at the shocked minion. "Like the boss said, no loose ends."

Between superspeed and a knuckle rap to the temple, Jamison was out cold on the floor in less than a second. A quick trip to the kitchen produced a couple of aprons. Steve used the strings of the protective garments to hogtie the minion.

Both the supervillain and Aisha would be expecting him back upstairs soon. Once again using his superspeed, and a little flight, Steve darted around the dining room as well as the rest of the restaurant, disabling the remaining explosives and disposing of the wires and circuit boards.

The problem was his bare chest. Maybe the truth would be best. Maybe he could cause a little dissension in the ranks.

Jamison groaned, and Steve paused. If he hauled the minion upstairs, he might reveal he was a super. Nope, better to leave Jamison down here and let the cops know where the jerk was after Rey, Aisha, and he dealt with the rest of the bad guys.

Steve slowed to the speed of the average citizen before he stepped out of the restaurant. The last thing he needed was to display his abilities on the security cameras that hadn't been disabled. Something poked his neck right below his jawline.

A woman's voice said, "Don't move, or I swear I'll cut you."

"I'm not moving," he said. But there was no one in his peripheral vision.

"You boys fighting over the spoils?" the female voice asked.

"Not exactly," Steve said. "Are you working for the terrorists upstairs?"

"What?" she exclaimed. "I'm not the one dressed like a minion."

Something about this didn't feel right. Maybe he should take a little bit of a chance. "I work for Winters & Franklin. They're a law firm in Canyon Pointe. You can video call them to confirm my identity."

"They represent superheroes, not supervillains," she said.

"Exactly."

"Do you have a phone," she asked.

"No," he lied.

Something vibrated in the pocket of the ridiculous elf shorts. What the hell? He'd turned it off before he and Aisha left Macy's. Unless Arthur or Tim had reactivated the vibration function for a reason . . .

Someone reached in his right shorts pocket. He tried to look down by moving only his eyes. The hand he could feel wasn't visible.

"Ms. Winters?" There was a slight pause before she added, "He claims he works for you."

The pokey object withdrew from Steve's throat. A woman faded into view. Her lithe figure was cloaked in a white unitard with a plunging neckline and matching boots. Her equally white hair was cut in a slanting forward design on the right and shaved on the left.

She smiled at him as she held out his phone. "Ms. Winters wants to talk to you."

Steve accepted the device and held it to his ear. "Hey, Harri."

"Aisha gave Jada her phone, and she apprised us of your plan." Harri took a breath before she rushed on. "Unfortunately, Glass is the only help you guys have right now. You need to take the bad guys down, and you need to do it fast. This supervillain is planning to kill the hostages."

"Not just the hostages." Steve fingered the melted edges of the huge hole in his shirt. "He plans to kill his thugs, too. Would you let the Atlanta PD know I've disabled the explosives I know of inside the restaurant underneath the courtyard? I stuffed the wires and circuitry into the planters. There may be more. Wait for my signal before setting off the apps."

Her breath whistled through the receiver. "It's being taken care of. By the way, thanks for not starting a super fight with Glass just to prove your manhood in the middle of a crisis."

He smiled. "You're welcome." He looked up at a nearby security camera. "I'm assuming you can see everything."

"Yep. Be careful upstairs. We'll vibrate your phone once before we activate the sonics."

"Thanks." He thumbed the icon to end the call and eyed the female super. "So you're Glass?"

"And you're the new Ghost Owl's sidekick?"

He grinned. "Not by choice. More like being in the wrong place at the wrong time." His smile faded as a worrisome thought occurred. "When you're in your glass form, how do sound waves affect you?"

"Let me guess." She crossed her arms. "Ghost Owl has a sonic death ray?"

"Not exactly, but you might want to stay flesh and blood." He waved his phone before he shoved it into his pocket. "There's an app on our phones that does emit an annoying high-pitched sound."

"Like a stun grenade?" Glass asked.

"Yeah." Steve started walking toward the nearest escalator, and she matched his stride. "We'll set them off at the same time in the courtyard. Can you take out the lookouts hiding behind the kiosks in the main hallway of the mall near Bloomingdale's?"

"No worries."

Except he was worried. He wasn't a hero. Not like Rey or Qiang or even Tim. He prayed he didn't screw up this rescue as he and Glass rode the escalator to the Main Level.

CHAPTER 30

Harri squeaked when the weapon pointed at little Jada. At someone she considered family. A scream threatened to follow the squeak out of her mouth.

Rey yanked Jada away from the muzzle of the weapon and jumped to his feet. Harri wanted him to grab Jada and Devon and fly the hell out of that damn mall. But if he did that, the other hostages would probably die. Rey was too honorable to let anything happen to anyone, but this was a situation where no matter how good and powerful a super he was, the odds were someone would get hurt.

Or die.

Her pulse pounded in her head as she watched the tense stand-off. Rey didn't make a move toward the minion, but she'd also never seen him so angry before. She crossed her fingers neither of the men would lose control.

Harri gasped. She couldn't seem to catch her breath. Did the Winters family have a history of heart problems? Given her parents' premature deaths, she'd never thought to ask.

Susan grabbed her left elbow. "Harri?"

Black spots danced before her eyes. She was going to watch Rey and Jada die on a live CCTV feed, and there wasn't a damn thing she could do. Just like Mom and Grandma Harri. She was losing her family all over again.

Strong arms caught her as she started to go down, but they were way too skinny to be Tim's. Tim always caught her when she couldn't keep her shit together.

When she let him anyway.

"She's hyperventilating." Miss Purrception's voice seemed to come very far away. "Tim, you two have any paper bags in this place?"

"Arthur, keep your eyes on that screen," Tim ordered. He hurried to the kitchen as best as he could after spending nearly two hours on his feet at Jeremy's party. Meanwhile, Miss Purrception practically carried Harri over to the recliner.

"Harri, are you having pain anywhere?" Susan asked.

"You doubt me?" Miss Purrception snapped while she settled Harri in the chair.

"Heart attacks in people our age aren't unheard of," Susan bit back.

"I'm not . . . having a . . . fucking . . . heart attack." Harri gasped between words. "Can't catch my breath—"

"Here, honey." Tim placed the opening of a brown paper bag over her mouth and nose. "Breathe into this." Harri grabbed the bag as if it were a lifeline. Anything to stop the horrified ache in her chest.

"You never called me honey," Miss Purrception said in a sulky tone.

"What?" Susan practically shouted in Harri's ear. By the time the new year rolled around, everybody in their circle would know about Tim's past romantic relationship with Miss Purrception. Actually, it kind of served him right.

Over the edge of the brown paper bag, Harri watched Susan's startled expression while her attention switched to Tim, then Miss Purrception, and back to Tim. It would be funny as hell if she could breathe properly enough to laugh.

Tim ignored the supervillain and called over his shoulder, "What's their status, Arthur?"

"Our unknown terrorist handed Devon over to the minion threatening Rey and Jada. He's now shaking Aisha's phone in Rey's face." Instead of his normal high-pitched squeak in a tight situation, Arthur sounded self-confident and grim.

"Where the hell is Glass?" Tim snapped.

"Unless Steve developed telekinesis, she's following him to the courtyard and taking out the lookouts." Arthur looked at the group hovering over Harri in the recliner. "I've got an idea to delay our unknown villain until Steve and Glass get there."

"Do it!" Harri and Tim said at the same time.

Okay, so maybe she should have lowered the bag from her mouth first.

Arthur's thumbs danced over his phone.

Harri dropped the hand holding the paper bag to her lap. "I need to see what's happening."

Tim helped her out of the chair. From Susan's mixed expression of perplexion and irritation, they'd be getting an earful once the current crisis was over.

Arthur moved to the middle of the couch so Harri and Tim could sit on either side of him. With her tiny turquoise cushions, it was a tight fit. Arthur tapped the "Send" icon with a decisive click of his thumbnail.

Their unknown villain's head jerked up and glared at the security camera. He lifted his free hand and shot the camera the bird.

Arthur's thumbs flew as he typed the next message:

Don't expect mercy. I don't play by the rules either.

At the top of the laptop screen, Steve entered the courtyard. Arthur tapped a key on the computer. On the screen, Steve jumped.

Arthur typed one more message to Aisha's phone:

Now, guess which one of us is the Ghost Owl.

The unknown villain's attention went from Rey's face to someone off screen. Probably Aisha.

Arthur hit the button on his laptop to activate the sonics app on all three cell phones.

CHAPTER 31

From the unknown supervillain's words and the appearance of Steve at the other end of the courtyard, someone back in Canyon Pointe was seriously messing with the villain via texts on her phone.

When his attention turned to her, Aisha lifted her hands and jerked to tear the scarf. She was ready for Arthur to activate the sonics on all three, but it still hurt like hell.

The pain didn't matter. Both she and Mister Spectacular surged to their feet and took out the closest minions.

Rey focused on the jerk holding Devon. The minion's weapon flew one way. The minion went the other. The father who had been behind them in line grabbed the weapon. He fired a plasma bolt over the heads of a couple of minions trying to run. The two bad guys tossed their weapons to the ground and went prone with their hands extended.

The parents also rose to their feet en masse. Some herded the kids toward the exits. Rey threw shoes with dangerous accuracy at the minions holding weapons on the child hostages. Other parents jumped the minions not engaging the supers. A handful went to aid the injured.

The whole battle was over in a matter of seconds.

All except their leader.

He lay on the floor and tried to shield his head from the well-aimed kicks of Jada and Devon. Rey pulled the kids off the unknown supervillain as Aisha and Mister Spectacular approached.

Aisha tried to subtly pick up her phone from the floor. She didn't succeed, not with her protruding abdomen. Jada leapt forward, grabbed the phone, and gave it to Aisha.

"Let's find out who you are," Mister Spectacular snarled. He reached down and ripped off the supervillain's mask. "Keith? Keith Oberton?"

"Wow, you recognized me." The supervillain sneered at the incredulous expression on Mister Spectacular's face. "I'm shocked."

"What the—" Mister Spectacular glanced at his audience and amended the word he was about to say. "—fudge, man?"

"You forgot about me." The supervillain wailed. Tears streamed down his face. "You said we'd be friends forever."

"Good grief, Keith!" Mister Spectacular threw his hands into the air. "Are you kidding me? We were in grade school! Couldn't you have just written to me or call me like a normal person?"

"How was I supposed to do that after you moved away? The letters I sent to your grandma's house were returned."

Aisha almost felt sorry for the man. He reminded her too much of Arthur. Would their firm's IT manager have ended up like this if Harri hadn't shown a little bit of pity when she was a Canyon Pointe city attorney and asked the judge for community service instead of jail time?

Mister Spectacular knelt beside Keith. "I'm sorry. The government hid us after the accident. Once I went public, you still could have—"

"How could I contact you? With all your publicists and lawyers? They never gave you my messages, did they?"

"It still doesn't give you the excuse for hurting people and threatening children," Rey snapped.

"Yeah!" Devon added with a scowl.

A woman in white unitard faded into view next to Rey and the kids, making all three jump. "G.O., you and your sidekick need to split. The police are about to enter." She held out her hand to Aisha. "I'm Glass. It's been a pleasure to work with you."

Keith's eyes widened. "Y-you're really the Ghost Owl?"

Before she could answer, Rey shot a nasty smile at him. "There's more than one of us."

The supervillain wannabe shivered as he stared at Rey.

That smile made Aisha shiver as well, and not in a good way. Ever since the incident with Professor Paranoia, something dark seemed to live inside her normally joyous husband.

"Santa?" Steve approached them. "We need to get to the reindeer now."

As much as she wanted to say something reassuring to her husband, niece and nephew, there was more she wanted to tell the crestfallen Mister Spectacular.

But she couldn't. Not in front of so many witnesses.

She turned and headed toward the main hallway. From the sounds behind her, Atlanta's finest rushed into the courtyard and started cuffing the minions.

However, she distinctly heard Devon say, "So, Mister Spectacular, what are you doing for Christmas? My grandma is an awesome cook."

Chapter 32

Steve swept Aisha into his arms despite her protests and zipped down the main hallway of the mall. They slipped inside Macy's, and he bent the gate back in place seconds before cops poured into the hallway from Neiman Marcus.

"Damn," Aisha muttered as they enter the supply closet/changing room. "We can't leave the Santa suit and elf costume here. Our DNA is all over them."

"That's your biggest worry?" Steve said as he ducked behind some boxes to change. "How do we get out of here without the cops thinking we're minions?"

Aisha laughed from the other side as the baby launched a sharp kick into her bladder. "I'm a minion with my bowl full of pro soccer player."

"If my nephew has his dad's powers, he's not going to be allowed to play pro sports." Steve tossed the ruined elf shirt to the floor. That had been one of his biggest regrets when he discovered his abilities. Not playing pro sports, but having to withdraw from the kids' teams he'd played in when he was ten. Even then, he'd known deep down it wasn't fair. Dad had been rather upset, but Steve had been too scared to tell him the real reason he'd quit.

"You okay?" Aisha asked.

"Sure. Why?"

"You get that same tone in your voice my husband's does when he's thinking about the past."

Steve wondered if Qiang would ever be able to read him the way Aisha could. Damn, he got that Qiang was being pulled in five different directions at once. Having Professor Paranoia fuck with his mind last spring didn't help his own insecurities, much less allow him to discover how to penetrate the prickly wall she'd placed around her heart after her husband died. He wanted to prove that he was someone she could depend on, but she hadn't even responded to the text saying he'd arrived in Atlanta.

He tugged on his jeans. "Aisha, can I ask you a rather personal question?"

She was silent for a long moment before she said. "Depends."

"How do I get Qiang to realize I'm serious about wanting to date her?"

"Wow, you don't ask the easy ones, do you?"

Steve pulled on his shirt and started to button it. "Look, I get she views me as a kid."

"Not as much as Harri does," Aisha said sarcastically.

"And Rey views her as a mother figure, too." Steve chuckled. "Did I do something incredibly stupid and/or cruel to Qiang when I was under Professor Paranoia's influence?"

"Not that I know of." An exasperated sigh punctuated another pause. "I hate to ask this, but when you're dressed, could you tie my shoes?"

"No problem." He tucked his shirttail into his jeans. "But can we go back to my situation?"

"You need to give her some time, Steve. You two technically only met three months ago. I know that seems like forever, but—"

"But it's not for you senior citizens," he quipped as he slipped on his loafers.

"Man, if you want to get laid, I would definitely not call the lady a senior citizen. It's creepy as well as insulting."

Steve circled around the boxes, knelt in front of Aisha, and started tying her left athletic shoe. "I get her reluctance to introduce me to her parents. They weren't super happy about her marrying a white guy. But how do I talk her into letting me get to know Connor one-on-one?"

"That's really going to take some time," she said. "You know how protective moms can be."

"True." He frowned as he tied the right shoe. "Aren't these Rey's footwear?"

"No," she bit out.

He stood. "It's okay if they are. It can't be any different the wearing his shirts."

"It is when my big honking women's size ten feet now can only fit into a men's size twelves."

"I thought comfort was the name of the game in your third trimester." She glared up at him.

"Never mind." He shrugged. "So what do we do with our disguises?"

As embarrassing as it was, Steve helped Aisha hide all the outfits except for the Santa suit's jacket under her clothes. Thank god, for stretchy pregnancy pants. She slung the Santa jacket over her shoulders. She also came up with a great cover story.

When the police found them, they didn't question Steve helping his very pregnant sister-in-law who was felled by Braxton-Hicks contractions during the evacuation. And the cops totally bought their story of hiding when they were locked inside of Macy's.

All except for one clever beat cop. She grilled Steve about where the Santa coat had come from. She wasn't buying that he found it on the floor inside Macy's. Luckily, Dennis, the mall's resident Santa Claus, rushed up and claimed he'd dropped the coat in the rush to escape with his elves.

However, Eric and Rey accompanying Dennis played up the anxious family members looking for Steve and Aisha. They tipped the scales in Steve and Aisha's favor. When a detective said Eric and Rey had already given statements, the cop rolled her eyes and finally let the matter go.

It was another two hours before they could get Eric's rental and head back to Betty and Marvin's place. Jada and Devon were in the third row, alternately babbling over the excitement and disappointment that they didn't get Mister Spectacular's autograph or a present for their expected cousin. Meanwhile, Aisha sat in the front passenger seat and conferred with Harri about the evening's excitement on her phone.

Steve pulled out his own phone and checked it again. Nothing.

Rey leaned over and whispered, "Just text her."

"And say what?"

"That you were thinking of her." Rey rolled his eyes.

"She hasn't answered my last couple of texts," Steve said. "I don't want to come across as needy. She's uncomfortable with the age difference as it is."

Aisha looked over her shoulder at him. "Qiang hasn't texted you because she's been at the hospital. Her mom had another stroke last night."

If he didn't feel weird and petty already, that news alone would have done it. "Is Hang going to be all right?"

"The doctors don't really know yet," Aisha said. "Even though Qiang got her to the hospital as fast as she could, this one was much worse than the last. The docs are warning Qiang her mom made be bedridden for the rest of her life."

"How's her dad taking this?" Steve leaned forward. "And Connor?"

"Connor's staying with Miguel for now." Aisha chuckled. "And Harri's got a plan to get Mr. Tranh over for Christmas dinner. It'll help that Susan's parents will be there."

"Susan's parents?" Rey interjected. "I thought her family were heading up to their cabin in the mountains."

"Long story." Aisha sighed. "The entire Kennedy clan is bunking at the Lechuza building for the holidays."

"Do we need to go back?" Rey asked.

Steve recognized the glint in his brother's eyes. He had the need to do something, anything, when someone else had a problem. Steve tried not to grimace. Rey's attitude made him realize how entitled he was. How blind Mom and Dad were to the real problems in the world.

Sure, they and his grandparents donated to various causes and volunteered their time on committees, but they didn't get their hands dirty. Not like Rey, who was taking his fortune he'd made on Captain Justice endorsements and sending his neighbors to school or bankrolling their small businesses.

Is that what Qiang saw in him? Both of her parents had been refugees when they came to the U.S. Maybe it was a good thing he hadn't gotten her a gift at Tiffany's. She'd probably think he was buying her affections.

"No, we don't need to go back to Canyon Pointe," Aisha said. "Harri's got everything under control."

"Who's cooking for all these folks?" Eric asked.

Aisha was silent for a long time until she murmured, "Harri is."

Both Rey and Eric burst out laughing.

"What's so funny?" Steve asked.

"Aunt Harri can't even boil water," Devon piped up from the back seat.

Chapter 33

In their bedroom, Harri could feel Tim staring at her from the bed though the lights were off. She climbed under the covers, but his body was stiff. And not in the fun, adult way.

She turned on her side. "Are we going to talk?"

"I can't believe you are letting her stay here," he muttered.

"Really? That's the way you want to play it?"

"You have no idea of how dangerous she is," he spat.

"I've got a pretty good idea she's up to something." Harri chuckled. "I just don't think either of us knows what it is yet."

"It sounds to me like she's dealing with unfinished business," he said.

"Are you upset that you're not part of the unfinished business she wants to deal with before she goes to prison?"

"You don't understand, Harri." Tim turned on his side to face her. The ambient light slipping past her blinds hid his expression in shadows, but his tone painted a pretty good picture in her mind. "Missy has never gone to prison without having an ulterior motive."

"I kind of got that from the NSB's dossier on her." She cupped his cheek. "But for Rue Liberty and the girls' sake, I'm going to deal with the hand I've got in front of me. You can't tell me if you had one last chance to make amends with Rebecca and Shane, you wouldn't take it in a heartbeat."

"That's different," he muttered.

"No," she said. "What's different are the paths each of you went down after Corvus took your families away from you. Just because she travelled the supervillain route doesn't mean she's totally irredeemable. Look at

Arthur. Besides, haven't you noticed Rey has a weird effect on everyone around him?"

He chuckled. "Point taken, but I still don't trust her. And I really don't get why you do."

"You mean, because she's your ex I should automatically be jealous?"

"Well . . . yeah."

"Uh-huh." Harri kissed him and patted his cheek. "I think you secretly want us to get into a naked pillow fight."

"You know I can hear you two," Miss Purrception called out from the living room. Tim had thrown a major hissy fit about her being in Steve's room, even though the Kennedy's were settled between Aisha's loft across the hall and Susan's apartment downstairs.

"Shut up and go to sleep, or I'll toss you out the window," Tim shouted.

"You hit it on the nose, Harri!" Miss Purrception laughed hysterically.

"Of all the—" Tim started to sit up, but Harri laid her index finger across his lips.

"Shut up and go to sleep, or I'll go get Susan to help me throw you out the window, too."

"Fine," he muttered against her skin. He wrapped his left arm around her as she curled up against his chest.

After the crazy day she'd had, Harri fell to sleep long before Miss Purrception stopped giggling on her living room couch.

⁕⁕⁕

Harri awoke to the smell of bacon frying. The spot next to her was cold and empty. Well, there was no shouting in her loft, so either Tim and Miss Purrception were behaving themselves or they were both lying dead on her living room floor. If the second option were true, maybe she should go rescue the bacon before it burned.

She rolled out of bed and pulled on her bathrobe before heading to the kitchen. To her surprise, it was Patty manning the frying pan. Miss

Purrception perched on a stool and sipped coffee from the aroma lying under savory smell of bacon.

"Good morning," they both said.

"Where's Tim?" Harri shuffled over to the cupboard and retrieved a mug.

Miss Purrception shrugged. "He got a message and took off."

Harri looked at Patty.

"NASA," she said as flipped perfectly crisped bacon onto a pile of paper towels on a plate.

"Are you shitting me? Don't they know it's Christmas Eve?" Harri reached for a slice of bacon only to have Patty smack her hand. "Hey! What was that for?"

"Let it cool. You'll burn your fingers and your mouth," Patty chided.

"Why are you practicing your mommyness on me instead of Grace?" Harri poured her coffee.

"Actually, she's babysitting me." Miss Purrfection smirked over the rim of her coffee cup.

The supervillain's statement was the first thing that made sense this morning. Harri retrieved the milk from her fridge and poured a dollop into her coffee.

Patty pulled a piece of paper from her jeans pocket. "This is for you. You wanna grab the eggs for me please?"

Harri took the folded note sheet, exchanged the milk for the eggs, and handed the carton to Patty before she read the message from Javier. "Wow." She looked at her assistant. "How'd Javier know what was on Qiang's shopping list?"

This time, Patty smirked. "Connor."

Harri frowned as she read through Javier's suggestions, mentally comparing them to the list Qiang had sent her yesterday. "Okay, this is going to be a balancing act between the kid's wishlist and what his mom thinks is appropriate. But the places to obtain said presents is helpful as hell."

"I can help you with the shopping," Miss Purrception volunteered. Again.

"Oh, hell no. You do not need to be seen in public until I've negotiated your surrender. Remember?" Harri ripped a page out of her domestic to-do notebook and started scribbling. "Here's your chore list to work on while I'm gone. And this is your down payment on legal services. Patty is not doing them."

"I'm not your servant." Miss Purrception's irritation was plain. "Patty could at least help me."

"Patty is making pies for tomorrow," Patty shot back. "And unless you want me to burn your eggs right now for getting mouthy with me, you will do your own damn chores."

The expression of shock on the beautiful supervillain's face was priceless. Apparently, few people told her no.

Harri grinned. "This is the woman who took on Black Death. My money's on her." She took a sip of her coffee and waited for the supervillain to make her move.

"Fine." Miss Purrception snatched the list out of Harri's hand. "I'll do it."

⁕⁂⁕

After breakfast, Harri drove toward the south end of Canyon Pointe. Despite Miss Purrception deliberately baiting Tim and being a generally annoying house guest, Harri kept to their agreement and stopped at Rue Liberty's house first.

Located in one of Canyon Pointe's older neighborhoods, the residence of Mrs. Margaret Reinhold was a classic 1930's bungalow with an addition on the back. Dormant flower beds guarded the sidewalk and red brick porch. The rest of the house was clapboard painted white with black trim around the windows. Icicle lights hung from the roof, and red and white lights wrapped the twisted pecan tree in the front yard like a peppermint stick.

Harri parked on the street and strode up the sidewalk. The door opened before she could knock.

"Harri!" Molly Reinhold, AKA the superhero Nix, enveloped her in a hug. The silver tinsel that was part of her black holiday sweater tickled Harri's nose. "What are you doing here?"

Nerves assaulted Harri full-force. "I need to talk to you and your family. Is everyone here?"

Molly waved for her to enter. "Of course."

Harri stepped into the house. A Christmas tree stood at the opposite end of the long living room from the unlit fireplace. Three red stockings hung from the mantel. Green and red hand-crocheted afghans covered the backs of the couch and armchairs. The place felt far cozier and friendlier than Dad's condo or Grandma Harri's mansion ever had.

Molly closed the door and led her to the kitchen. A half-consumed pan of cinnamon rolls sat in the middle of the kitchen table. Their warm scent filled the air. From the used dishes, the ladies had just finished their breakfast. Both Rue and Kerry rose from their chairs.

"Harri?" Rue Liberty's voice quavered. "What's so important that couldn't wait until tomorrow?"

"A new client has requested to meet with you, Kerry, and Molly," Harri forced out. "You might want to sit down for this."

Kerry's face hardened. "Mom."

"Yes." Not knowing what to do with them, Harri shoved her hands into her jacket pockets.

Rue slowly sat down. "Why now?"

"Honestly, I think Rey got her heart to thaw." Harri shrugged. "She would like to meet with you three to make amends before she turns herself into the authorities. If you're willing, that is."

"Sure she's turning herself in," Kerry scoffed. "She's just conning you, Harri."

"What if she's telling the truth?" Molly's glittery eyes glistened.

"Where?" Rue asked softly. Her hands trembled on her lap. It was the first time Harri really noticed how translucent the retired superhero's blue-veined, wrinkled skin was. Rue Liberty had always seemed so damn strong. That she'd live forever.

Now, she was simply an elderly woman wondering if she could make peace with her estranged daughter. Harri's heart broke for both Rue Liberty and herself. She would have done anything to make up with her father if he wanted to go straight and sober.

"Java Joe's." Harri rocked on her heels and pulled out the slip of paper with the real location and handed it to Rue. The older woman read it and nodded.

"I told her this is totally up to you guys," Harri continued. "I'm not forcing you. Nor will she be allowed at Christmas dinner tomorrow."

"Because if she shows up, I'll throw her off the roof of the Lechuza Building myself," Kerry growled.

"Kerry!" Molly's expression was a mix of shock and anger.

"Sweetheart, I don't expect you to forgive your mother, and I don't expect you to go, but I want to see my daughter one last time." Rue's glare brooked no disagreement from her granddaughter.

Molly lifted her chin. "Well, I'm going with Grandmother no matter what you think."

Kerry shook her head. "I think you're all suffering from holiday wishful thinking."

"All right, but I'm telling you three the same thing I have already told Miss Purrception." Harri met each of the superheroes' gazes. "If you turn this meeting into a super brawl, I will press charges on all of you."

"No problem," Molly said cheerfully.

Rue murmured her consent, but it was Kerry who worried Harri the most.

The woman couldn't roll her eyes in a conventional way, not with her full gold-green irises and cat pupils, but she conveyed her reluctant resignation. "Fine. We'll meet with Mom."

"Where is she right now?" Rue asked.

Harri glanced around the small, cozy kitchen. Mindful of Miss Purrception's admission, she asked, "When was the last time you had you home and car swept for bugs?"

The older woman inclined her head. "Understood. How about we swing by Java Joe's at three this afternoon?" However, she held up her index finger.

Harri nodded at the real time. "Works for me. See you all later."

As she climbed into her car, she wondered if she was doing the right thing by all of her firm's clients. This meeting could be a wonderful thing for the Reinholds. Or it could be worse than the hostage situation Aisha had found herself last night.

CHAPTER 34

Aisha tried not to grimace like Mom was as Devon regaled everyone at brunch with another rendition of last night's events. Aunt Queenie appropriately gasped and clapped at the right moments. Dad kept eyeing her over his coffee, probably wondering if she'd lost her damn mind.

Part of Aisha didn't want to ruin what was left of her nephew's childhood enthusiasm. The other part wanted to shake him and force him to face reality. Both Devon and Jada had been very close to getting killed last night. According to the news, two of the folks hit by the plasma weapons the villains had been carrying were lucky to get away with burns and contusions, but the third person was still in critical condition at one of the local hospitals.

A knock on the front door brought Devon's rendition to a screeching halt. Mom started to rise, but Aisha patted her hand.

"Stay here, Mom. I'm closer and it's probably just one of the neighbors." Aisha scooched her chair back and stood. She needed to move around anyway. Her lower back ached something fierce from being in one position for too long.

Through the antique stained glass windows framing the doorjamb, she could make out a white man in dark clothes. She strode to the door and opened it.

Familiarity flooded her. Mister Spectacular's cool blue eyes and dark hair were unmistakable. However, he was dressed in civilian clothes, black jeans and the red and black jersey of Atlanta's pro football team. He held a large manila envelope in his hands.

"Hi, um, I know this is a little awkward—"

"How did you find us?" A bit of worry and irritation tinted her voice.

"The police witness reports from last night." Pink flooded his cheeks and ears. "Your nephew—"

Aisha couldn't help chuckling as she remembered what Devon had done. "Well, he did invite you over for Christmas."

Mister Spectacular's own laugh was self-deprecating. "Well, I wanted to thank you for your assistance last night, too. And I owe your nephew an autographed photo." He held out the manila envelope and lowered his voice. "I've been making the rounds to all the kids' homes this morning. Their lives were put in jeopardy just because they attended my event."

He shrugged. "It's just I figured I'd better approach your parents' house as a civilian."

"Why don't you give it to him yourself?" She smiled and gestured for the superhero to enter.

Mister Spectacular stepped inside the house. "I also wanted to let your brothers-in-law know the inside elf on the hostage event didn't get away. He was arrested early this morning."

"That's a bit of a relief." Aisha called out, "Devon! There's someone here to see you!"

Her nephew raced into the hallway from the dining room and skidded on Mom's freshly polished hardwood floor. His eyes widened as he took in who was standing beside her.

"M-Mister Spectacular? I-I didn't think you'd really come."

"You stood in line for a long time just to meet me." Mister Spectacular held out the manila envelope. "This was the least I could do after everything that happened last night."

Devon accepted the envelope. "Wow! Thanks! You've got to come in and meet everybody." He grabbed Mister Spectacular's left hand and tugged him toward the dining room. "Are you hungry? We're just eating breakfast even though it's lunchtime for Grandma and Grandpa because we all slept in after everything that happened last night. Jada wanted to get a picture of us with Santa Claus for Aisha and Rey's baby because we live in Portland and they live in Canyon Pointe. Jada wants to go to a different mall today, but Mom's scared of letting us go out again. Hey, everybody! This is Mister Spectacular!"

Aisha couldn't help laughing. Would her own baby be that exuberant in ten years? Better yet, would she be able to keep up with him? Hell, Devon wasn't even a super, and he wore her out.

When she followed the superhero and her nephew into the dining room, Dad was directing Eric where to put an extra chair while Mom fetched another place setting from the kitchen.

⸺⸱⸱⸱⸺

After the table was cleared and the first round of dishes loaded into the dishwasher, Jada nagged LaShun to go to another mall for pictures. Devon was torn between the agreed-upon present and his desire to hero-worship Mister Spectacular. The superhero mollified him by saying he wouldn't leave until they got back from their errand because family and Christmas were important.

Apparently, the rest of the family had picked up on Mister Spectacular's desire to talk to Aisha, Rey, and Steve alone. Well, everyone except Aunt Queenie. Mom and Dad went out with Eric, LaShun, and the kids to the mall with the promise to pick up pizza on the way home.

"Pizza for Christmas Eve dinner?" Mister Spectacular asked after the rest of the family trooped out the back door and bundled into the rental SUV. He and the twins helped Aisha clear the counters while Aunt Queenie presumed to supervise from her chair at the kitchen table.

Aisha laughed. "It's a tradition. Mom managed a pizza shop here in Atlanta while Dad was working on his PhD when my siblings and I were little. She tried to give most of her staff Christmas Eve off, which meant she brought home pizzas for dinner that night."

"You should stay for dinner," Aunt Queenie said. She leaned over in her chair and slapped the superhero on the rear end when he passed her carrying a stack of plates and silverware. "You could put some meat on those bones."

Mister Spectacular's mouth fell open at her brazen behavior, but he froze, obviously not knowing what to do.

"Aunt Queenie!" Aisha glared at her elderly relative. "I swear I'm going to tell Eugene to stick you in a home!"

"Good!" Aunt Queenie peered over the rims of her spectacles. "A lot of those orderlies are Rey and Steve's age." She cackled. "In fact, I'm going to take a nap. I'll need my energy to sexually harass the rest home's staff."

Aisha shook her head as her great-aunt shuffled out of the kitchen with her cane. "I'm so sorry about that, Mister Spectacular."

"I'm not." Steve grinned. "She's not checking out my ass anymore."

"Let's get some drinks and go into the living room," Rey suggested. He turned to Mister Spectacular. "You obviously have a lot of questions."

Once they poured sodas or, in Aisha's case, apple juice, the four of them retreated to the family room.

"First of all, my name is Lane. It's less of a mouthful than my moniker." Mister Spectacular set his soda on a coaster. "I'm not sure where to start."

"Mind if I ask you one first?" Aisha said.

Lane sighed. "You want to know about Keith."

She nodded.

"He was my best friend in grade school. Back when I was still normal." A wistful expression crossed Lane's face. "After the accident, my grandmother was scared. Hell, I was scared. Of what I was becoming. What I could do." His gaze met hers. "I was a ten-year-old kid, and I was—"

"Preoccupied," Aisha said.

"A selfish brat," Lane said.

"You're putting too much on a ten-year-old's shoulders," Steve said. He shook his head. "Frankly, so is Keith. He's blaming you for abandoning him how many decades ago? The man needs psychiatric help. And you don't need the guilt."

"It sounds like you know what you're talking about." Lane smiled.

"I was the same age when I found out that I was a super." Steve shrugged. "I was too afraid to tell my parents because I was adopted."

Lane's eyebrows rose. "I rather got the impression you two were identical twins."

Rey snorted. "Not that identical."

"Lane, why don't you start with the questions you wanted to ask last night?" Aisha said.

He turned to her with a bemused expression. "What the hell made you decide to use the Ghost Owl moniker?"

She and Rey exchanged looks before Rey turned to Lane and said, "Because I didn't want it."

❦

Over the course of the next couple of hours, they were up front with Mister Spectacular. Or as upfront as they could be about Corvus and Professor Paranoia. Not so much about Tim.

Mom and Dad brought pizza home, and Mister Spectacular agreed to stay for Christmas Eve dinner. That promise was enough to get Devon to run upstairs with Jada to wrap their gift for the baby. It also brought out Devon's superhero card collection.

Thankfully, Aunt Queenie behaved herself for the rest of the evening. It was also obvious Lane was reluctant to leave. Mom picked up on it and invited him to tomorrow's dinner.

Once Lane left, Devon looked up at Aisha. "Martin and Renata are going to totally freak when they get here tomorrow and see Mister Spectacular at the table."

"Devon, maybe you should chill about Lane's secret identity," Eric said. "Yeah, we've got supers in the family, but that doesn't mean you should be outing anybody, especially that Lane is Mister Spectacular. That's his decision."

"But Da-a-ad, he's friends with Aisha and Rey and—"

"And we've had the discussion about talking about your aunt and uncle in public," Eric said sternly. "More than once."

"Yes, sir."

Aisha hated seeing the dejected look on Devon's face, but Eric was right. She rubbed her belly. It would be hard enough when her son developed his own abilities. Her eyes burned at the difficulties her son would face in life. He would never be normal.

"I think I'm going to bed," she said.

"You feeling okay, baby girl?" Dad peered at her intently through his glasses.

"Just tired between yesterday's excitement and my third trimester." She smiled and patted her belly. "Junior's quiet, so I should grab some sleep while I can."

"I'm coming with you," Rey said.

The sounds of the family discussing Mister Spectacular's visit followed them up the stairs.

"Are you really okay?" Rey looked worried as he closed the bedroom door.

"Scout's honor, I'm fine. Just tired" Aisha kicked off her shoes.

"Can I run a possible moniker past you?" he asked as he pulled off his high-tops.

"Sure." Curiosity filled her, and she crossed her fingers he'd come up with something good. She was so tired of fighting with Harri about the subject.

"What about Black Falcon?" Rey watched her with a hint of worry.

"*Black* Falcon?" Aisha raised an eyebrow.

"Don't go there." He pulled his shirt over his head and tossed it on the antique rocking chair. "It's not used on the NSB registry. I checked."

"That doesn't mean it hasn't been trademarked, but I'll run the check when we get home." It was good to hear Rey enthusiastic about this again. After everything that had happened with Professor Paranoia, she had wondered if he really wanted to return to the hero business. Especially after all his delays over the last three months while Reuben taught him how to run Marta's kitchen.

"So you like the name?" Rey seemed a hair anxious about her approval.

"Love it, honey." She smiled brightly. "I'm so used to teasing Harri about race. I'm sorry if I came across as dismissive."

"I was thinking about asking Jeremy to design something in black with red accents. Would you be upset if I used a visor similar to Ghost Owl's?"

"Of course not." She laid her blouse on top of the hope chest.

"What about a similar costume design as well?"

"You want his and hers super outfits?"

"Actually, I want to avoid the tights." Rey waved his hands. "I totally understand why Tim didn't use them. Lycra Kevlar is rather . . . constrictive."

She pointedly looked at his jeans and grinned. "I can understand that."

"So . . ." he drawled.

She raised her head. Rey looked at her expectantly.

"So, I'm really glad you came up with something." Aisha laughed. "You would not believe some of the monikers Harri was pitching. I love her, but she has no clue when it comes to branding." She bit her lip, but she needed to know. "Can I ask why the visor?"

He unbuttoned his jeans. "Because Molly says my eyes give me away." He stepped out of each leg. "And she isn't the only one to say that to me. But I want to wear a visor to protect Steve. I respect his choice not to enter the hero business, but the two of us wearing the same face puts him in danger if I don't cover my features fully."

Rey rubbed his hand over his beard. "The facial hair doesn't exactly do a good enough job.

Aisha nodded as she tried to unhook her bra. "That's totally logical."

"You sound surprised," he said dryly.

"No, I'm sorry, I'm—" Frustration welled out of her. She could take out supervillains, but her inability to do something as simple as removing her bra without ruining it while pregnant drove her insane.

"Let me." He crossed to her and turned her around. "Don't need Momma Bear getting grouchy tonight."

Once he removed the offending garment, she pivoted and played with his beard. "If that's the case, maybe your new moniker should be Daddy Bear."

He wrapped his arms around her and laughed. "If we did, the only endorsement I'd get would be from Redwood's contacts in the adult industry."

"Not a good idea." She grinned and threw her arms around his neck. "I don't like sharing my toys."

"That's a very naughty thing to say on Christmas Eve," he murmured.

Yep, Molly was right. Rey's golden eyes were a dead giveaway. Aisha found herself sinking into their depths.

"Then maybe I need to show you how naughty I can be." She followed with a soul searing kiss.

If someone had told her last Christmas she'd be married and expecting now, she would have referred them to a psychologist on her contact list. But now, she had everything she ever dreamed of, so she'd revel in her Christmas miracles and worry about the rest next year.

CHAPTER 35

At twenty past one in the firm's conference room, Harri wanted to smack Miss Purrception. Her fingernails tapping the rhythm of the William Tell Overture on the table over and over again was getting on her last nerve. That one nerve was already frying because Rue Liberty was never late.

"Why can't we open the blinds?" Miss Purrception whined.

Harri clenched her fists on her lap. "Because we don't want anyone else to know you're here."

"There aren't any windows looking into the Lechuza Building from the building next door," Miss Purrception said as she twirled around on her chair. Of course, the supervillain had totally cased the place.

Harri would've been disappointed if Miss Purrception hadn't. "Because there's still enough space between the buildings for someone to slip back here and see you."

Miss Purrception pitched forward, her head hitting the maple veneer with a thump. "I can't handle this waiting."

No shit. Harri kept herself from saying the phrase out loud. It wasn't professional, and as a private practicer, clients are what kept the lights on. No matter how annoying they could be.

At the ring of the side door buzzer, both women jumped to their feet.

"Sit down," Harri ordered.

"They're my family," Miss Purrception snapped.

"And they're my clients," Harri shot back. "Their wellbeing is my priority." She gave Miss Purrception a vicious smile. "Besides, your ex-boyfriend is looking for an excuse to Tase your ass."

The supervillain pursed her lips and lowered said ass back down into her chair.

Harri stalked out of the conference room and to the side door leading to the Lechuza Building's parking garage. The smell of espresso filled the reception area. Patty had already jumped on making everyone's drinks at the sound of the buzzer. They wouldn't have been able to keep their firm going without her. Harri wondered if she shouldn't slip some extra money into their assistant's gift envelope.

When she deactivated the security system and opened the side door, there had obviously been a family fracas on the way from the looks on the three women's faces. Harri held up a hand.

But before she could say anything, Rue Liberty said, "We worked it out in the car. Both girls promise to behave themselves."

"You had better." Harri scowled at the younger women. "I've got a chief of security itching to Tase a Reinhold."

That statement seemed to shock the twins out of whatever they'd argued about on the way here. They exchanged looks before Kerry asked, "Why would Tim want to Tase our mom?"

"Because the Ghost Owl and Miss Purrfection used to be a thing decades ago." Harri waved a hand. Even Rue Liberty was surprised by that admission. "Now, get in here because it's expensive enough to heat this damn building."

Molly brought up the rear of the trio. She paused next to Harri. "Tim's not our dad, is he?"

"You can ask for a DNA test, but I'm pretty sure he's not." Harri closed the door and reset the security system.

"How do you know Mom didn't lie about it?" Kerry asked.

"Because one—" Harri held up her right index finger. "—according to them both, they weren't an item until after his murder trial, and two—" She raised her middle finger. "My boyfriend wouldn't have cheated on his wife." She pointed her fingers at the twins. "You two are only three years younger than Shane would be if he were still alive. Now, come on before your mom starts climbing the walls."

The Reinhold women followed Harri into the conference room. Miss Purrception rose slowly to her feet. "Hey, girls. Mother."

Molly rushed around the huge table and threw her arms around her mother. "I missed you so much."

"I missed you, too." Miss Purrception stroked her daughter's short platinum blond bob. "What did you do to your hair?"

"Harri's stylist suggested the cut and color as part of my brand make-over." The younger woman's face fell. "You don't like it?"

"It's adorable." Miss Purrception smiled.

Rue Liberty stepped toward her daughter as Miss Purrception and Molly parted. "I'm glad you came home for Christmas, Monica."

"So am I." Miss Purrception swallowed hard. "Thank you for watching out for the girls all these years."

After they hugged, the rest of the Reinhold women looked at Kerry.

"Is Tim our dad?" the young woman spat.

"No." Miss Purrception shook her head. "I didn't meet him until after I lost custody of you and Molly."

"If you want to kiss and make up, then you need to spill," Kerry growled.

Damn. After this morning's talk, Harri had been sure the super could hold her anger. Kerry was usually the more level-headed of the fraternal twins. But not knowing who her biological father was had gnawed a hole through whatever patience she had.

Miss Purrception sank into the closest chair. She rested her elbows on the table and clasped her hands so tightly together, her knuckles shone white through her skin. "It's not that simple, sweetie."

"Looks pretty binary to me." Kerry said and crossed her arms.

"He'll never acknowledge you and Molly." Miss Purrception shook her head sadly. "He's married."

Harri bit her lower lip. This was terribly personal. Even as the ladies' attorney, she wondered at the ethics of seeing their family drama, up close and personal.

"You're afraid of some supervillain's wife?" Kerry looked incredulously at her mother.

"No." Miss Purrception sucked in a deep breath. "It's more like guilt. I didn't know he was married when I slept with him, and his wife is a sweet lady. She doesn't deserved the grief."

"You chose a stranger over your own daughters?" The hurt in Kerry's voice made Harri tear up herself.

Something Aisha said after returning from Japan stuck in Harri's mind. Miss Purrception had made some comment to Aisha about how she was surprised Captain Mojave had given up his obsession with capturing the Ghost Owl. Everything clicked, like a freakin' snapshot. A love triangle. All of this grief was over a freakin' love triangle.

But before she could say anything, Patty entered the conference room with a tray full of coffee cups.

"Ladies, may I offer a bit of personal advice after having been knocked up by a so-called hero myself?" she said as she handed out everyone's drinks. However, her attention was solely on Miss Purrception.

The supervillain frowned, but she nodded.

"I understand wanting to protect your children from pain, Missy. I really do," Patty said gently. "But my daughter Grace has the right to know about her dad, no matter how much of a shit Black Death is. Sourpuss and Nix are smart ladies. They'll see the truth."

Patty sighed and set the tray on the table. "And frankly, if we can figure out who the twins' dad is, they will, too. Eventually. Once their anger and fear stop blinding them."

Kerry stared at Patty. "You know?"

Patty shrugged. "Well, everyone here except Tim figured it out. But he's a little blind himself when it comes to your mom. She broke his heart, though he'll never admit it. Not to mention, it took years and Harri to repair it."

The supervillain stared at the top of her coffee cup. Harri counted to ten before she broke the silence.

"The ball's in your court, Monica." Harri gestured at Kerry. "You're the one who said you wanted to make amends with your family."

Slowly, Miss Purrception raised her head. "Your father is Captain Mojave."

A myriad of emotions flashed over Kerry's face before she laughed long and hard.

"That dick? He hit on me!" She collapsed into the chair next to Harri. "No wonder he freaked out when he learned who I was."

Molly stared at her sister. "He didn't!"

"Yep." Kerry shook her head, still chuckling. "This was before you decided to take the plunge, Molls."

"I ought to—" Miss Purrception started to rise.

"No, sweetheart." Rue Liberty pressed her hand to her daughter's shoulder. The elderly superhero looked ready to give Captain Mojave a beat down herself. "There's other ways to deal with him."

Kerry looked up at Harri. "Would it be all right if we use your conference room to talk for a while?"

"And maybe could Mom come to dinner tomorrow?" Molly asked with a tentative, worried sound in her voice.

"Let's see how you four do for the next hour or two." Harri used her index finger to indicate all the Reinhold women. "If you four don't trash my conference room, then you're all welcome to Christmas dinner."

She grabbed her cup, and Patty the tray. They left the conference room, and Harri closed the door behind them. There was still some tension in the ladies' voices, but maybe she just needed faith the Reinhold family could work out some of their issues before Miss Purrception turned herself in to the authorities.

"You did a good thing in there," Patty said softly.

"No, you did." Harri bumped Patty's shoulder with hers. "Have you thought about going to law school yourself?"

"Nah. I'm satisfied being a paralegal." Patty smiled. "And by the time Steve's done with law school, Grace will be walking and potty-trained. She'll need me a lot more, and you can't afford to have both Steve and I in school at the same time. Do you really trust Arthur or Tim to handle the phone lines?"

"Denying your own gratification for motherhood?" Harri teased.

"No, I simply don't need the headaches. Besides—" A sly smile crossed Patty's face. "You couldn't run this place without me."

"True, but according to the firm handbook, I have to at least pretend to promote your employee advancement."

They both laughed at Harri's piss-poor joke until they reached the elevator.

"Seriously though," Harri said once they were inside the car and climbing toward the fourth floor. "What about getting your mediation certificate? The state doesn't require a law degree for that, and the firm will cover the cost of those classes."

"That would be doable." Patty nodded thoughtfully.

The scent of cinnamon and nutmeg mixed with yeast filled the air as the elevator groaned to a halt. The doors to all the apartments on the fourth floor stood open.

"Did you start the baking without me?" Harri asked.

"No." Patty frowned. "Susan asked if she could use my kitchen to prep lunch for her family. She said she didn't want her mom to jump in the middle of everything."

They entered Patty and Arthur's apartment. Susan and her niece Audra looked a little surprised to see them.

And Harri could see why. The thirteen-year-old was rolling out pie dough while Susan peeled an apple.

"What the devil are you doing?" Harri jammed her fists on her hips.

"Helping out a little since you were kind enough to shelter us in your building instead of kicking us out to your stable." Susan grinned.

"But I was going to make the pies!" Harri protested.

"No worries, Miz Winters!" Audra grinned. "We got this covered. The pumpkin pies are already in the oven, and the bread for both breakfast and dinner are rising."

"Breakfast bread?" Patty asked.

"My grandmother's stollen recipe," Susan said while she cored the apple. "It's a German tradition." She waved her knife in the air. "Don't worry. We've got a couple of loaves of plain white from Betty's recipe rising, too."

"Wait a minute!" Harri stomped over to the island where Susan was slicing up the apple. "How'd you get Betty's recipes?"

"I had Arthur pull them off your e-mail account." Susan pointed the knife in Harri's direction. "And before you start yelling at him, I convinced him it was for a good cause. You were reuniting a family downstairs. That took priority over cooking for all of us."

"I guess I can go upstairs and start on the cookies." Harri dropped her hands to her sides.

Susan winced. "Uh, Mom and Tracy already got a jump on those in my kitchen."

"You can go help them frost the cookies," Audra offered.

"Sounds like the Kennedys have the baking under control." Harri smiled at the teenager despite her disappointment in not getting to use Betty's recipes herself. Susan and her family were only trying to help. "I'm sure there's some prep work I can find in my own kitchen."

Harri's smile faded as she realized what was missing in the apartment. "Where's Arthur and Grace?"

Patty shrugged. "He said they were helping Tim downstairs with his project."

Well, that was peachy. Harri needed to have a talk with her boyfriend about letting her staff have time off during the holidays.

She eschewed the elevator and jogged up the flight of stairs to her loft. With tomorrow's massive dinner, she needed all the exercise she could get.

Harri tapped in her code on the keypad and yanked on the handle of the rolling door. It didn't budge. Was she that tired and stressed that she typed in the wrong code?

She tapped it in again. No luck. And she could definitely hear male voices on the other side of the door.

She tried her numbers for the third time. The door still didn't budge. She beat on the reclaimed wood. "Who the fuck changed my PIN code?"

The inside lock slid back and the door rolled open a couple of inches. One of Francisco's big brown eyes peered up at her.

"That is inappropriate language around a baby, Ms. Harri," he chided.

She crossed her arms and glared at the boy. "Why have you locked me out of my own home?"

"Sorry, honey!" Tim called from somewhere inside. "That's my fault. I told Francisco to guard the door."

"Go back downstairs with the cooking ladies," Francisco ordered.

"I have to . . . use the bathroom," she amended. "I'm not going to make it back downstairs in time."

Francisco's eyes narrowed. "Then go use Ms. Aisha's bathroom. We've got a top secret project going on in here, and you can't come in."

A horrible scenario built itself in her mind's eye. "Timothy Mitchell Canyon, you'd damn well better not be working on the NASA spacesuit in my living area!"

"Language, Miss Harri!" Francisco shot her an appalled look.

"We're not!" Tim yelled.

She heard male laughter, which only brought her blood to a boil.

"Honey, go chill at Aisha's for a bit," Tim yelled. "We'll let you know when you can come back."

On that note, Francisco slammed the loft door shut and locked it.

"Oh, for the love of . . ." Harri rubbed her temples. The beginning of a stress headache hammered on her brain.

Nothing was going as she planned. All she wanted for Christmas was a perfect family holiday for Grace. Was that too much to ask?

CHAPTER 36

Steve slipped into the family room while Aisha and Rey retired for the night and everyone else marveled over Mister Spectacular's visit. He pulled out his phone. Still no text from Qiang, even though he'd asked about her mom. He was half-tempted to call Harri or Patty to make sure something worse hadn't happened.

Aunt Queenie tottered into the room, her cane in one hand, two glass tumblers rattling in her other, and a good-sized bulge in the right pocket of her sweater. "Take these," she ordered.

Steve grabbed the tumblers before they slipped from her grasp.

"Sit 'em on the coffee table," she commanded.

"Yes, ma'am." He placed the tumblers where he was told. "Do you need anything else?"

"Yeah." She jabbed her cane at the couch. "Sit your own ass down, son. We need to have a chat." She slowly, and painfully from her expression, lowered herself into the closest armchair.

"A chat about what?" After some of her earlier comments and actions, he was a little nervous about being alone with the elderly lady.

She pulled a nearly full bottle of bourbon out of her pocket and held it out to him. "Why don't you be a gentleman and pour?"

"Are you sure we should be doing this?"

Aunt Queenie eyed him. "You're twenty-one, right? A shot of bourbon ain't gonna hurt you none." She chuckled. "Betty gets on her high horse about my drinking, but I don't have too many pleasures left in this world."

Steve poured two fingers in each glass and set the bottle between them. He handed a tumbler to Aunt Queenie. "Cheers."

They clinked their glasses together and took a sip. Steve's eyes watered at the burning sensation in his throat. He'd never been a big drinker in college despite the urgings of various roommates. Part of his reluctance was the fear of losing control and outing himself as a super. After watching his roommates' hangovers, consuming alcohol to the point of puking never made much sense to him.

"Call her," Aunt Queenie said.

"Who?"

"The girl you're expecting to hear from."

Steve shook his head. "That's not a good idea."

"Why not? Because it means you're making a commitment?"

"It's not that—"

"You can't let fear rule you, Stephen." Aunt Queenie watched him over the top of her spectacles. "If I'd waited for my chance at love like everyone said I should, I wouldn't have my Eugene. And I treasure the few months I had with my Stoney because we lived it to our fullest." She took another sip of her bourbon before she added, "You wait too long and this girl will slip right out of your life, never knowing how you feel."

"It's a little more complicated than just her and me."

"She married?"

"Widowed." Steve set his tumbler on a coaster and scrubbed his face with his hands. "Her son's special needs, and her parents live with her because she's taking care of them. Her mom had another stroke yesterday. She's got her plate full between working two jobs and her family."

"Then she needs to hear directly from you," Aunt Queenie said. "None of this texting crap. A voice soothes a soul in a way emojis can't." She tossed back the rest of her drink, set aside the tumbler, and forced herself to her feet. "I'll give you some privacy. Like I said, don't wait too long, Stephen. Love is something you need to grab when it's in front of you."

Steve smiled. "Thank you, Aunt Queenie."

"Just clean up for me." She patted his shoulder as she shuffled past him and out of the family room.

He pulled out his phone once again. Still no text from Qiang. It took a deep breath and the rest of the bourbon in his tumbler to tap the "Call" icon on his screen.

The line rang once. Twice. When he was on the verge of hanging up, Qiang said, "Hello?"

"It's Steve." He stood and started pacing. "I wanted to make sure you're okay. Harri told us about your mom being back in the hospital."

"I'm fine." Cloth rustled in the background. "I just got home a bit ago and got Dad to bed."

"I'm sorry. It's got to be pretty rough for both of you."

"Yeah, I don't know what I'd do without Miguel and Harri right now."

Steve winced. Not him. Because he came to Atlanta for the holidays. He should have stayed in Canyon Pointe. He cleared his throat.

"I take it Miguel's been watching Connor for you."

"Yeah." A yawn came through the receiver. "Look, Steve—"

"You're exhausted and getting ready to head to bed." The words seemed to rush out of him. "I just wanted to let you know I was thinking of you."

"Steve," Qiang said softly. "You're a wonderful guy, but things between us aren't going to work. I've got my parents and son, and you'll be starting law school in a couple of weeks. Neither of us are going to have time for anything more in our lives."

"But—"

"You'll meet someone. Maybe a classmate. Or maybe someone at a concert or ballgame. Or something. Take care of yourself." The line went dead.

For a brief instant, he had the urge to throw his phone through the wall. Instead, he sat on the couch once again, leaned back, and stared at the plaster on the ceiling while his heart ached.

There had to be a way to convince Qiang there was more to life than taking care of everybody but herself. Even though her strength was one of the things he found attractive in her, he wanted to be the one to take care of her when she needed it. And from the exhaustion in her voice, she definitely needed it.

He was headed back to Canyon Pointe in three days. Maybe he could come up with a plan to convince her to let him into her life.

CHAPTER 37

It was still dark outside when Aisha woke up to the sounds of excited kids downstairs. It almost felt like past Christmases when Grams and Pawpaw were both still living in this house.

"Merry Christmas," Rey murmured in her ear. "Just think. In a couple of years, our son will join in the chaos."

Her laugh turned into a grunt as her son launched on hell of a kick into her diaphragm.

Rey laid his right hand on her bulge and smiled. "He's definitely active this morning."

"I think he's experiencing his first case of FOMO."

"FOMO?"

Sometimes, she forgot how much pop culture he missed, growing up on the streets. "Fear of missing out."

The baby batted at Rey's hand. He leaned over and murmured in Spanish, "Hey there, little one. Don't give your mama a hard time. You'll be here soon enough."

The activity in her abdomen immediately calmed down. Aisha breathed a little sigh of relief.

"I really wish I knew how you did that."

"Let's hope it lasts after he's born." Rey pulled her tight against him. "We really need to decide on his name."

A shriek from Devon echoed through the old Victorian. Aisha giggled.

"I think he found our present."

"And you're changing the subject again," Rey whispered against her hair.

"I get that you respect my dad, honey, but when someone says 'Marvin', I automatically hear 'The Martian.'"

"Then what about Miguel Mitchell Garcia Franklin."

She rolled the name through her mind. Even Dad had objected when she'd brought up naming the baby after him.

"Baby girl," he'd said. "I know Rey wants my respect. But damn, he's already got that. A man should name his son after his own father, not his father-in-law."

But the combination of Miguel and Tim's would definitely meet Dad's criteria. Besides, the kid would never find pens or cups with Hunahpu on them.

"What if we switch it to Mitchell Miguel Garcia Franklin?" She rubbed Rey's hand. "That flows a little better."

"More branding to make our son popular to the widest customer base possible?"

Aisha groaned. She had said almost the exact same words on the day Harri had first brought Rey to Aisha's old office.

"Fine. We'll name the next one Arthur," he teased.

She looked up at Rey. "Can I deliver the first one before you start planning the next one?"

"I just want Baby Mitch to have a sibling he can get to know in their childhood."

Feet pounded up the stairs. LaShun's voice penetrated the walls. "Go wake up Aisha and Rey. I need five more minutes."

"Three, two, one," Rey murmured. Their bedroom door crashed open.

"Merry Christmas!" Jada and Devon shouted before they jumped on the bed.

"You sure you want more?" Aisha teased.

"Lots more." Rey grinned.

CHAPTER 38

At mid-morning on Christmas, Harri slipped out of her loft and headed down to her office. All she managed to do for this afternoon's feast was get up at seven a.m. in order to put the ham into her own damn oven.

After Miss Purrception had beaten her to the kitchen and prepped the ham with pineapple and cloves. The rest of the Reinhold family arrived a half hour later. They split into teams to cook the potatoes and two different types of stuffing.

Susan's mom had already stuck the turkey in their oven downstairs. She insisted on also making the gravy, saying this was probably the last Christmas she'd be able to cook. Harri couldn't argue with her request.

Arthur handled the vegetables. Susan's sister Tracy did the hors d'oeuvres with the assistance of her kids.

Poor Marta arrived early, probably thinking she would bully Harri out of the kitchen. Instead, Miguel ensconced on Marta on Harri's overstuffed chair and waited on her, hand and foot. Marta's son and daughters engaged Miguel's boys and Connor in a massive gaming competition.

Harri stared at the phone on her desk. This was a call she didn't want to make. Not after seeing Miss Purrception trying so hard to be part of her family again. But even as they worked on the ham together, the supervillain said she was keeping her promise to turn herself in for Harri's help in reuniting with her mother and daughters.

Harri hit the button for her ex-husband's cell number. It only rang once.

"Yeah," Eddie's voice came over the line.

"I need your help."

In the background, she could hear him tell Sarah he needed to take this call because it was work. There was a whoosh before Eddie growled, "Why the hell are you calling me on fucking Christmas?"

She bit back the sarcastic remark that struggled to escape. Instead, she said, "I wouldn't have, but this is for a client."

An exasperated sound echoed through the receiver. "Who needs to be bailed out?"

"I need you to contact someone you trust at the NSB." She tapped her pen on her desk. "Miss Purrception wants to turn herself in."

"What?"

"Tomorrow morning," Harri added. "Miss Purrception wants to turn herself in."

"Since when do you represent supervillains?"

"This is an exception," she replied.

"Where is she right now?"

Harri sighed. "You know I won't answer that. I want her to live long enough to surrender."

Eddie grunted. "Bring her to my office at nine a.m. sharp. Otherwise, I will raid the Lechuza Building and charge you with obstruction. You got me?"

"Five by five."

"And, Harri?"

"Yeah."

Eddie's voice softened. "Merry Christmas."

"Merry Christmas to you, too." She smiled to herself. "See you in the morning."

She tapped the button to end the first call and hit the speed dial for Aisha's cell phone.

"Happy Holidays, Harri!" Her partner's cheerful voice rang through the receiver. An instant later, a chorus of voices called out greetings. Aisha laughed and said, "Give me a second."

The background hubbub died down.

"What's up?"

"You liberal heathen," Harri teased. "I can't believe you didn't say 'Merry Christmas'!"

"You didn't say 'Happy Kwanzaa' either, conservative bitch."

They both laughed, but it quickly died into an uncomfortable silence.

"The arrangements have been made," Harri said.

"If this is what Monica wanted, why do you sound so damn guilty?"

Harri leaned back in her office chair. "Because I feel like I'm giving Kerry and Molly their mom, only to yank her away again."

"Look, I like Monica, too," Aisha said. "But she made her own decisions, as poor as some of them were. If she does her time and behaves herself, she'll be out in a couple of years."

"I think I'm more worried about Kerry confronting Captain Mojave."

"Wait." Aisha's voice grew concerned. "She found out?"

"Monica finally came clean." Harri chuckled. "Everyone kept pointing the finger at Tim."

"Oh, geez!" Aisha laughed. "He would've made a much better father. Actually, you might want to have him talk to Kerry. He's been a pretty good sounding board with Arthur, Rey, and Steve."

"That's a good idea." Harri swallowed the emotions threatening to clog her sinuses. "I'll see you in a couple of days." She was finally realizing what bugged her. Part of her was hoping the girls were Tim's daughters so she could be their stepmom. That was truly the stupidest thing she'd ever wanted, and the best at the same time.

"You okay?"

"Yeah. The whole situation is bittersweet."

"Merry Christmas, Harri."

"Merry Christmas, Aisha."

The side door buzzed the instant Harri hung up the phone. She jogged out of her office and to the garage entrance. Jeremy and Leonardo waited outside with brown paper bags and a little red wagon full of alcohol bottles.

She cocked her head. "Leftovers from the salon Christmas party?"

"One can never let top shelf liquors go to waste," Leonard said primly as he air-kissed her.

"Why aren't you upstairs?" Jeremy eyed her.

"I got kicked out of my own kitchen," she said through gritted teeth.

"Oh, thank god!" Jeremy dramatically held his hand over his heart.

Harri's mouth fell open. "What's that supposed to mean?"

Jeremy set down his bags and framed her face with both palms. "It means dinner will be edible because, Harri, darling, as much as we love you, you cannot cook."

CHAPTER 39

At five minutes to midnight on New Year's Eve, Steve stood on the cell phone patio nearest to the ICU and texted Qiang. The weather reports claimed Canyon Pointe would get its first snowfall of the season, and the air had the sharp nippy promise of it, but nothing was happening yet.

A minute later, she charged through the doorway. "This isn't a good time, Steve." She scowled up at him.

"Both your mom and your dad are asleep, and this will only take a minute," he said.

"Look—" She waved her right hand for emphasis. "—you're a great person, but I've got my hands full at the moment."

"I know, and I hear you." He took the small box he'd carried back from Atlanta out of his jacket pocket. "This is part of your Christmas present. The other part is tomorrow. You and your dad can sleep in because I'll be here with your mom. All day. You both need the break. Once school starts back up for both me and Connor, I can take him and pick him up."

"Look, I really appreciate this, but . . ."

"But what?" he asked.

When she didn't speak or move, he took her right hand, placed the box in her palm, and curled her fingers around it. "Call me when you're ready to add the last charm. I can wait.

"I—" she started, but he silenced her with a very thorough kiss. One that left her breathless.

No one had kissed her like that in almost five years. Not since the night Kevin died.

"Happy New Year, Qiang." Steve smiled at her again before he leapt into the crisp air and flew out of sight.

Her fingers trembled as she opened the gift box. A silver charm bracelet sat on white velvet. Six charms were already attached, profile silhouettes with birthstones where the eyes should be and names engraved. One each for Mom, Dad, Connor, and even Kevin. The fifth charm was a tiny calculator. She had to smile at the sixth charm—the Sparx lightning bolt.

Qiang had balked at the cosmetics line one of Nix's endorsees had tried to pitch her, but Aisha said something feminine wouldn't hurt her brand. They'd finally agreed to try out a small, tasteful jewelry line. It figured Steve would use the lightning bolt charm to represent that part of her life in a subtle way.

Finally, pinned to the top right corner was a seventh charm. Steve's. Not part of her circle yet, but close by.

He said he was willing to wait.

Qiang stared in the direction Steve had flown, but he was long out of sight. The only things in the sky were snowflakes as they swirled through the air. Maybe he really did understand the weight on her shoulders right now.

The bells of the churches started to toll the hour. In the distance, fireworks colored the snowflakes at the lakefront celebration. A new year. The city covered in a pristine blanket of white to represent the start of the calendar. And maybe, something new to warm her heart, too.

CHAPTER 40

Two months later . . .

Wearing her orange prison jumpsuit and white slip-on shoes, Monica waited patiently in her cell as the two guards cuffed her wrists and ankles. The other three aimed their Tasers at her through the bars. Their fear tickled her funny bone. If they only knew that Byron S. Trubble saved their asses from a kicking. She needed to behave herself in order to stay in the general population of Mauvaises Prison where Trubble currently resided. It was the only way to complete her mission.

She shuffled out of her cell as ordered by the deputy warden. The man was little more than a bureaucrat, not a warrior, hiding behind the other men. He'd be the one to take hostage if things went south.

The guards locked the collar around her throat and attached the control poles. A little guilt troubled her as they marched her down the aisle to the jeers of the other prisoners, but the feeling had more to do with lying to Harri than any of the multitude of crimes she'd been accused of. Or committed.

Damn, for a former city attorney, that woman was nearly as naïve as Rey Garcia. At least the kid had the excuse of being younger than Monica's own daughters. But if she told Harri what was really going on, the attorney and her little army would do something noble.

And really, really stupid.

Monica and her guards reached the private consultation room. The place smelled like piss. They locked her ankles to the chair and her wrists to the table before they unhooked the control poles from her collar. The idea was she couldn't leave without dragging all the furniture out of the room with her.

Idiots made her laugh.

The guards left the room. They made her wait another ten minutes before they allowed Carol Inunza into the windowless, bare consultation room. Carol sat on the one remaining chair on the opposite side of the table and said nothing until the door locked behind the guards and the two of them were alone.

"I heard you got into a scuffle during the exercise hour."

"Nothing I couldn't handle." Monica smirked. "These idiots think because I haven't been charged with murder I'm incapable of killing."

"You didn't—" Carol said.

"There's only one person here I want to kill, and I rather enjoy seeing him behind bars."

"Anything to report yet?"

"It's only been two weeks." Monica rolled her eyes. "I told you it would take longer than that to get what we need. He knows who I am, and he has no reason to trust me. Yet."

"We're still sticking to our regular schedule." Carol had the don't-argue-with-your-mom expression and voice down pat. It may even work with her husband's family as well as hostile witnesses on the stand, but Monica merely smiled.

"It's your time to waste," she said.

"What's that supposed to mean?" Carol's eyes narrowed.

"I'm not staying here a minute longer than I have to. Once I have the goods, I'm out of here." Monica leaned over the table. "Sooner if I have to. I already lost my daughters because of these assholes. If I get a hint of them going after any of kids, whether living in the Lechuza Building or not, well . . ." She straightened and shot Carol a malicious grin. "I know where to hide the bodies."

Coming in June! New challenges await our heroes when the legal team of Winters & Franklin find themselves defending America's greatest superhero after a tragedy in San Francisco results in a horrible death toll. Are Harri and Aisha representing the worst mass murderer in U.S. history? Or is Ultramegaperson the pawn in someone else's game?

Turn the page for a sneak preview of *Hero De Jure*!

Hero De Jure

©2019, Suzan Harden

"Harri!"

Patty Ames's shriek proceeded her bursting through Harri Winters' office door. "You've got to see this!" She rushed to Harri's second hand maple desk and grabbed the TV remote, her pale face even whiter than usual.

The Action 12! News logo flashed in the bottom right corner of the supersize screen hanging on the wall opposite from Harri's desk. A panoramic view of San Francisco Bay and the Golden Gate Bridge filled the screen. The bridge glowed under the rising sun.

Until a dark blur hit the north end of the city's famous landmark.

Cables snapped and flailed. Bits and pieces fell, but from the distant perspective, they were probably slabs of pavement and chunks of metal larger than Harri's ancient Honda. Vehicles tumbled hundreds of feet into the vicious Bay current. Harri covered her mouth with her hand to keep from screaming as well. They were watching innocent commuters plunging to their deaths. Even if every super in California and the surrounding states had been there, they couldn't have saved everyone.

Aisha, Susan, and Arthur darted into Harri's office and stared at the TV screen, no doubt their attention drawn by Patty's shriek.

"... current death toll is unknown. The damage to the San Francisco icon allegedly happened during a battle between Ultramegaperson and Doctor Liquidation that started at the San Francisco Federal Reserve." The camera shot switched to evening co-anchor Essie Morales in the studio. This level of carnage required someone with poise, which Essie had in spades. Nella Lopez, the senior producer of Action 12!'s news division, must have called all hands on deck early this morning.

Essie's concerned-journalist expression was firmly fixed on her beautiful face. "Ultramegaperson is assisting the Coast Guard in rescue efforts. Guy Montana, spokesman for the National Security Bureau, says a thorough investigation will be undertaken once all victims have been retrieved.

"In other news, the Dow Jones—"

"Victims retrieved" was reporter-speak for an obscene number of deaths.

Patty hit the mute button and set the remote back on Harri's desk. "You want me to call them."

Harri wearily shook her head. "No. Ultramegaperson will call us when they're able. No comment until we decide how we need to spin this."

The law firm's assistant nodded. Before she could take a step, the phone lines at her desk started ringing at once. Patti rolled her eyes.

"What a way to start a Monday morning." She strode out of Harri's office.

"Arthur—"

"On it. I'll see what information I can retrieve." Arthur Drallhickey, the firm's head of IT and a reformed supervillain himself, charged out the office door. If anyone could dig through the bureaucratic bullshit and learn the truth, it was him. Harri ignored the fact that some of his techniques weren't exactly ethical.

"You two have any bright ideas?" Harri leaned her right elbow on the desktop, set her chin on her palm, and stared at her legal partners.

Aisha Franklin shook her head. "We need more information first." She gestured toward the TV screen which was replaying the top news story after Essie's brief update on the other headlines. "What hit the bridge?"

"Considering its size, it wasn't a person." Susan Kennedy watched the replay closely. Harri had hired their former law school classmate nearly a year ago to cover for Aisha during her maternity leave. Susan had an excellent legal mind, a ton of trial experience, and was pretty damn patient considering the chaos Harri and Aisha's personal lives had been during the initial months Susan was with them. She'd become a valued part of the team, which was why they'd offered her a partnership.

Out in the reception area, Harri could hear Patty repeating, "No comment," like it was a Buddhist mantra.

Aisha stalked over to Harri's office door and closed it. "Now's when I really wish I could drink coffee again."

"Wean Mitch early." Harri grinned at her partner.

"Your godson's only four months old." Aisha gave her a dirty look. "He's not even eating solids yet."

"But is he flying yet?" Harri continued to tease.

If Aisha had laser vision, Harri would have been a crispy critter.

"When you two are finished bickering—" Susan started to say, but Harri's intercom buzzed, interrupting her.

Patty wouldn't interrupt them unless this was super important.

Harri poked the appropriate button on her phone set. "Yes?"

"Nella is on line one," Patty chirped.

"I'll handle Nella. Transfer her to my office, Patty." Aisha strode toward the office door. "Find out what hit the Golden Gate Bridge, and you'd better hope it wasn't something our client actually did." She left, closing the door once again.

No doubt Nella was hoping to finagle an exclusive out of Aisha. Harri would be the first to admit her best friend was better at handling the publicity side of their boutique clientele.

"She's right." Susan snatched the remote and thumbed the slow-motion button as Action 12! News began to replay their film of the morning's incident for the fourth time.

Ultramegaperson could be the biggest twat waffle on the planet, but they had come through when Aisha needed some help last Christmas. And the fees from the trans superhero alone kept the firm afloat this year while they rebooted Rey's career.

The intercom buzzed again, and Harri tapped the button. "Yeah, Patty?"

"Ultramegaperson is on line two."

Harri hit the speaker function. "Hey, Ultra! Susan's here with me. What do you need from us?"

"Um, Harri," the superhero said hesitantly. "This is really bad. I'm under arrest."

Hero De Jure is currently available for preorder at your favorite retailers!

Acknowledgements

To be frank, I wasn't expecting the 888-555-HERO series to take hold with people the way it has. Let's face facts. This is a pretty unconventional superhero series. I want to extend many, MANY thanks to the readers for taking Harri, Aisha, and their family, friends, and associates into your hearts.

A ton of gratitude goes to Jaye Manus of QA Productions and Elaina Lee of For the Muse Design for making my books look so professional.

Additional recognition goes to my fellow writers Angela Penrose, Joseph Bradshire, Scott Dyson, Val St Crowe, and Kirsten Harrell for their cheerleading.

Once again, *gracias* to all of my attorney friends, whose wild stories may or may not have been used in these books.

And most of all, to Darling Husband, Genius Kid, and Princess Bella. I love you all so much.

About the Author

Suzan Harden is a recovering attorney who writes fiction to regain her sanity. She currently lives in the Great Lakes region with a husband who believes writing is a practical career option and a kid who thinks she's too enamored with superheroes.

www.ingramcontent.com/pod-product-compliance
Lightning Source LLC
Chambersburg PA
CBHW070959180726
48291CB00004B/1358